W9-DDL-226

PAT RANDOLPH—her worst nightmare was coming true before her very eyes. Could she do anything to stop the tragedy of her life?

RACHEL CORY—she held the fate of Iris Delaney in her hands. All she had to do was tell Robert what she knew. But did she have the right to destroy someone else's marriage?

ROBERT DELANEY—he demanded answers from Clarice and was determined not to be put off any longer. Could he bully her into submission?

———————————

Series Story Editor **Mary Ann Cooper** is America's foremost soap opera expert. She writes the nationally syndicated column *Speaking of Soaps*, is a major contributor to soap opera magazines, and has appeared on numerous radio and television talk shows.

Cordelia Burke is a novelist who lives in New York City with her husband and young son. She has been a loyal fan of ANOTHER WORLD since the series began.

Dear Friend,

Pioneer Communications Network takes great pride in presenting the eighth book in the Soaps & Serials paperback series. If this is your first Soaps & Serials book, you're in for a pleasant surprise. Our books give you a glimpse into the past, featuring some of the most exciting stories in the history of television soaps. For those of you who are old friends of the Soaps & Serials line, thanks for your support.

Here's one of the many questions we've received from our thoughtful and loyal fans. A reader from Owensboro, Kentucky, wondered if the Ewing family on ANOTHER WORLD got their name from DALLAS—or was it the other way around? Both producers swear that the use of the Ewing name was strictly coincidental. It must be noted, however, that Larry Ewing on ANOTHER WORLD was around long before J.R. and his family made the scene on DALLAS.

Although we can't answer all of the letters we receive, we still enjoy hearing from you. Keep writing!

For Soaps & Serials books,

Mary Ann Cooper

Mary Ann Cooper

P.S. If you missed previous Soaps & Serials books and can't find them in your local book source, please see the order form inserted in this book.

ANOTHER WORLD

8

HAUNTED BY THE PAST

Soaps™ & Serials

PIONEER COMMUNICATIONS NETWORK, INC.

Haunted by the Past

ANOTHER WORLD paperback novels are published and distributed by Pioneer Communications Network, Inc.

SOAPS & SERIALS™ is a trademark of Pioneer Communications Network, Inc.

ISBN: 0-916217-38-8

Printed in Canada

10 9 8 7 6 5 4 3 2 1

HAUNTED BY THE PAST

Chapter One

An Unanswered Question

Waiting for a young couple to make up their minds about breakfast, Clarice Hobson pushed aside a lock of her curly blond hair with the pencil she had poised above her order pad. She was just about to make a suggestion when she heard someone pounding on the window of the diner. As she casually looked up to see who it was, her heart jumped into her throat. It wasn't just an impatient trucker who wanted a quick fill-up at the pump, as she had assumed. It was Robert Delaney.

Trying to contain her fear, Clarice quickly took the order and then walked to the diner's entrance. Robert had been her boyfriend until he married someone else, not knowing she was pregnant. All through her pregnancy Clarice had kept her secret, but now, from the look on Robert's face, she guessed that he suspected the truth.

Desperately, she hoped her guess was wrong. She tried not to think of the consequences if it wasn't. Her happiness, even the safety of herself and her baby, Cory, now several months old, depended on Robert's not knowing.

Robert burst through the door. "Clarice, I have to talk to you," he demanded. "Now."

She watched as a look of vehemence transformed the face she had once loved so well. It was a noble face with a strong brow, straight nose and a full-lipped mouth, now tight with anger. His wavy brown hair was disheveled and mussed as if he'd been raking his fingers through it over and over again.

Glancing around the diner and noticing the curious looks of the people there, she quickly nodded her head.

"Yes, I'll talk to you," she said with all the calmness she could muster. "But not here." She pointed in the direction of the hallway that led to the kitchen, and when she went that way herself, he followed close at her heels.

Once they were alone in the hall, she turned and said, "I thought you were still on your honeymoon."

Robert and his new wife, Iris, had been on a cruise for several months. It had been Iris's wedding present to her new husband. It had also conveniently removed him from Bay City, which, Clarice suspected, had been Iris's main motive for taking the trip.

"I just got back the other day," he replied, not able to meet her eyes.

He feels guilty, she thought to herself, *and why shouldn't he?* Once Iris had decided she wanted him to herself, she had been swift in alienating him from Clarice. One day she and Robert were lovers, and the next he barely had time to speak to her. But Clarice doubted that he even had an inkling of how he had been taken over by Iris. She supposed he just thought she had fallen head over heels in love with him.

Clarice watched Robert shift uneasily from foot to foot until he burst out with his next words.

"Look, I didn't come here to discuss my honeymoon," he barked and then caught her eyes with a hard stare. "I've just seen Cory."

With a sinking feeling in the pit of her stomach Clarice realized her worst fear was coming true. She said nothing.

"Now do you know why I'm here?" he challenged.

She ignored his question. "How did you see him? He's with Ada."

"Ada was at Mac and Rachel Cory's. I stopped by to say hello this morning."

Robert still couldn't get over the events of that morning. He had driven to his new father-in-law's home to drop off his stepson, and had decided to say hello to Mac and Rachel himself. He had been surprised to find Rachel's mother, Ada, playing with a young baby. When he'd asked whose baby the boy was, Ada had cleared her throat and looked uncomfortable. Then, staring directly into his eyes, she had stated flatly that he was Clarice's.

The impact of her three simple words had felt like a punch to his stomach. Ada was saying much more than the child was Clarice's: the infant was *his*, too. His own son. And when he had looked at the young child closer he had become more positive that his suspicion was true. Even at such a tender age, Cory was so like him, anyone would have to be blind not to see the resemblance. Now he was gazing at Cory's mother, his hard eyes demanding her to respond.

She fought to control her trembling. "What were you doing with my baby?" she finally asked.

"Our baby, you mean," he declared. "Yours *and* mine."

He watched the reaction on her face. Clarice was a simple woman. Though not unintelligent, she had none of the sophistication of his new wife, and the lack of it made her a bad liar. He'd always been able to read her emotions just from looking at her face. But her face said what her own voice denied.

"Your baby? He's not your baby. He's my baby." Her eyes refused to meet his.

"Clarice," he began, sarcasm entering his voice, "the simple facts of biology decree that a baby has to have both a mother *and* a father."

She stepped away from him. "I know that," she said stubbornly. "But you're not Cory's father."

"What about all those times we made love? Isn't that where babies come from?" He hated to badger her this way. He didn't like to see the fear in her eyes that his questioning seemed to produce, and he wondered what it was that she was so fearful of. But if he had a son, dammit, he wanted to know. Determined, he approached her and yanked at her elbow, turning her to face him. "If I'm not Cory's father," he asked angrily, "then who is?"

"No one," she insisted, then seeing his raised eyebrow added, "No one you know."

He let go of her elbow with an angry snap. "I'm his father," he persisted. "I know it."

"You don't know anything," she retorted. "His father is—" She tried to think

11

fast. "His father is someone I only knew for a short time. He left me before I could tell him."

At least that much was true. She could take some comfort in not being a complete liar. She once had tried to tell him about their child but he had been rushing off to do something with Iris. He'd even brushed off her plea for just a little time alone with him.

"You expect me to believe that? When did you have time for another man when you were with me? I would have known." He looked insulted.

"There are lots of things you don't know, Robert Delaney," she huffed.

Thinking back, Clarice remembered that before she ever got the chance to speak with him again, Iris had paid her a visit. In a heated confrontation, Iris had warned her that if she ever told Robert that he was the father of her baby, she'd stop at nothing to destroy her life. Hadn't she even tried to buy Clarice off with a blank check to get her out of the way?

Clarice knew she was no match for her. Iris, rich and beautiful, was an expert at manipulating people to do her bidding. She also suspected that Iris didn't make empty threats. If Clarice ever told him that Cory was his, Iris probably *would* destroy her life. Now that she had a young child dependent on her she couldn't take that risk. She didn't doubt Iris would go to any length to get what she wanted.

"I don't know why you won't tell me that Cory is mine," he finally said, interrupting her thoughts of the past, "but I know he is."

Clarice just shook her head and stared at her scuffed waitress's shoes. If only things were different. . . .

"I know he is," he repeated, "and I'll prove it." He started to leave.

She placed a shy hand on his sleeve to stop him, but he shook it off.

"I mean it, Clarice. Cory is mine. I won't have you keep me from him."

"This has nothing to do with you, Robert," Clarice said softly. "It's not your business."

"It is my business," he said with more fortitude than he felt at the moment, his anger softened by Clarice's obvious distress. "And I'll make it my business until I discover the truth."

With that, he turned and left.

Clarice leaned against the wall and wondered how it could be that her life had just been turned upside down by one angry confrontation, which had taken hardly more than five minutes.

As she returned to her customers she looked out the plate-glass window and saw Robert getting back into his car.

"Good luck, Robert," she whispered to

him under her breath as tears began to form in her eyes. She had no doubt that he would accomplish everything that he had threatened. She only hoped that the truth wouldn't destroy him . . . as well as herself.

On the other side of town that evening Rachel Cory sat propped up in bed, having just put aside a novel she'd been trying to concentrate on. All evening she'd been waiting for this moment, and now that she could hear Mac finishing up his nightly ritual in his dressing room, she knew it wouldn't be long before she'd be able to tell him what had been, until this afternoon, only a delicious suspicion.

She looked around their bedroom and was pleased with what she saw. Decorated in peach and beige, it was the kind of room that made a person feel calm and happy. She had decorated it herself, one of the first projects she had taken on when she had married Mac and moved to the Cory mansion. As a child, she had peered at the house in wonder and had always wanted to live in it, but she had never, even in her happiest dreams, thought she would.

Now she was mistress of the house, safe and content in the warmth of Mac's love and her love for him. With a sigh she thought of how her life had been before she met Mac and how he had helped her become the person she had wanted so desperately to be. Once she had been envious and, yes, she had to admit to herself, cruel when her envy of other people's happiness made her strike out at them in anger.

But Mac's love had changed her. She was truly happy now and had no need to interfere in other people's lives. Mac's patient understanding and encouragement had let her relax and let the goodness she had never known was there inside, blossom. And now, something else was blossoming within her.

She smiled when Mac opened his dressing room door and entered the room.

"You look like the cat who swallowed the canary," he said as he crossed to their bed and sat on the edge of it next to her. "Is it the book?" He picked it up and placed it on the end table.

Rachel shook her head, her smile spreading across her face.

"What is it, then?" He took her chin in his hand and gave it a playful tap with his forefinger. "A surprise?"

Rachel watched as the lines around his eyes crinkled in expectation. She loved his face. Not classically handsome but craggy, with a strong nose and a high brow, it was the face of a man who had seen and done many things and yet had still kept his youthfulness and a zest for life. Mac was a

15

strong man, but a tender one, too. It was the tenderness that made him so dear to her.

"A wonderful surprise," she said, her eyes bright in a lovely oval face framed by dark hair.

Mac pushed a wave of it back from her cheek. "Let's see now, what could be a wonderful surprise?" He thought for a minute. "Is it a present?" Mac and Rachel often bought each other presents for no other reason than that they wanted to please each other.

She began to shake her head, but then caught herself. After all, what could possibly be a better present than this surprise? She changed the shake to a nod.

"Oh, good, I love presents. Let's see." He stroked his chin. "I'll ask the traditional question. Is it bigger than a breadbox?"

Rachel laughed. Unintentionally, he was making this game a lot of fun. "Not at first. Not now, at any rate." She placed her hands on her still flat stomach.

Now he looked really puzzled. "So it gets bigger, does it? I know! You've bought me a plant!" It was the best he could do.

"Mac, when would I ever buy you a plant?" she exclaimed and laughed. "You would never remember to water it." He was notoriously absentminded.

"Well, if you bought me one as a special

present I might," he insisted, fingering a piece of lace that bordered her nightgown. "I guess I give up," he conceded, frowning. But then his face brightened. "Why don't you just give me my present now," he said with a devilish grin.

"I can't," she said. "It isn't ready yet."

He tugged at her arm playfully. "Then why bother to tell me. You're being such a tease!"

"It won't be ready for around seven or eight months, Mac."

He was beginning to regard her with a funny look in his eyes.

"They take nine months, you know." She was unable to contain the smile that seemed to overtake her whole face.

"Rachel," Mac exclaimed, "you don't mean . . ."

She nodded. "I'm going to have a baby, Mac. The doctor told me today."

"And you waited all evening to tell me?" He jumped up. "Why didn't you tell me as soon as you heard?"

She laughed. "Well, first of all I didn't want to interrupt you at work because once you heard you would have told everyone there right away, and I wouldn't have had anyone to tell myself."

He sat back down again next to her and she poked him playfully in the ribs.

"And secondly, I wanted to wait until we were alone, and since my mom and

Jamie were both at dinner and Mom insisted on staying until Jamie went to bed so she could read him his favorite story, and then insisted on staying even later so she could tell us how he already knows the story by heart and hardly even needs to have her read it to him anymore—"

Mac put up his hand. "I get the picture."

"So you see, I didn't have a chance until now to tell you."

He wrapped her hand within his two strong ones. "Dear Rachel," he murmured. "I couldn't be happier."

Her eyes shone.

He pulled down the covers and got into bed with her. He plumped up some pillows, then put them behind his back and stretched his arms behind his head. "Let's think of some names."

"If it's a boy I was thinking of Mackenzie, after you," Rachel suggested, nestling her head against his chest.

"That's such a big name for such a little baby, and really, all the men in my family have always been Mackenzie. I think it's time to break tradition. How about Edward? I think that's a fine name."

She wrinkled her nose. "The only Edward I ever knew was a boy who used to pull my hair and call me skinny-bones."

Mac laughed. "He must have been in love with you, my dear."

"I don't care," she protested.

"All right, not Edward, then."

"If it's a girl, I like Victoria."

"Victoria Cory," he mused. "I rather like that. It almost rhymes."

Rachel snuggled against his chest as he wrapped his arms around her.

"But whatever the name is he or she is going to be a very lucky child to have such a beautiful mother."

"And a smart father," Rachel added.

"And all the love in the world."

She nodded happily in agreement.

"Ah, Rachel," he sighed, pulling her closer after he had turned off the light. "You've made me such a happy man."

"And I'm happier than I ever thought I could be," she said, turning her face to his for the kiss she knew was waiting.

There wasn't anything that could spoil this new happiness, she thought. At last, her life was as perfect as any life could be.

Chapter Two
A Secret Engagement

Marianne Randolph leaped from the couch at the first ring of the telephone. She didn't want anyone else to answer it.

"Hello," she answered nervously, after she had grabbed the receiver.

"Miss Randolph?"

It was Dr. Gilchrist's receptionist, just as she'd thought.

"Yes, did you get the test back?" Marianne asked eagerly. Her palms were so moist with anxiety she could barely hold on to the receiver.

"It's positive," the receptionist said matter-of-factly.

Marianne had no reply. Her worst fear had just been confirmed. She was pregnant.

"Miss Randolph, you'll need to make an appointment with the doctor. Will next week be soon enough?"

In a daze Marianne made the appointment, and then hung up the phone. Slowly she walked over to the couch and collapsed. How could this be happening to her?

She'd always been such a sensible young woman, her life following the course her parents had expected; then she fell in love with Chris Peterson. As her feelings for him became more powerful than her common sense, she soon found herself doing things she had never thought she would do.

She could count on one hand the number of times they'd made love. Each time it had been so spontaneous, so right and natural, she hadn't thought of protecting herself. Chris certainly hadn't, either. In fact, he had been the one who had always encouraged them to live for the moment, and pretend the future didn't even exist.

Well, that wasn't possible now. If only she could pretend she wasn't pregnant. . . . But here she was, barely out of high school with a baby on the way. Suddenly, the future she'd once pretended hadn't existed didn't seem as bright as she'd always assumed it would be.

"Marianne?" Pat Randolph called to her daughter as she came down the stairs. "Who was that on the phone?"

She entered the living room. A tall woman with lovely blond hair and an oval face with a sweet, pointed chin, she was as gentle and well-mannered as she appeared to be. Marianne and her twin brother, Michael, were the lights of her life. She doted on them.

Quickly, Marianne brushed aside the nervous tears that had begun to course down her cheeks. She couldn't let her mother see her this way. She turned, making her face as clear of care as she could muster, and lied. "It was Chris. He wants me to meet him at his office for lunch."

"How nice," Pat responded. If she were being honest with Marianne she wouldn't have expressed her approval. In truth, she didn't really like Chris Peterson. He was nice enough, but he never seemed at ease in her presence, and she wondered what it was that made him so uncomfortable. Did he have something to hide?

But for Marianne's sake, and because she strove not to interfere in her children's lives, Pat pretended to be happy about her daughter's relationship with him. Marianne was still young enough, she reasoned, to make a few mistakes in her choice of men without them being harmful.

"That's why I have to run," Marianne announced, edging around her mother to grab her handbag from the table next to the stairs. "I'm late."

Pat took one look at her daughter's face, and then placed a restraining hand on her arm. "Is there something wrong, darling? You seem upset." She scanned Marianne's face even closer. It was so like hers in some ways. The same open blue eyes and high brow, the same generous mouth that smiled readily. The only part of it that was like her father was a square, determined jaw. Today, however, the jaw wasn't so determined-looking, and her eyes and mouth seemed sad and troubled.

Marianne shook her head. She couldn't speak or she'd risk breaking down and telling her mother the news. She wasn't ready to do that yet. She wasn't ready for the disappointment she knew she'd see in her mother's face.

Pat brushed aside a lock of Marianne's blond hair that had fallen across her forehead. "Are you positive?" she asked softly. Something *was* bothering her daughter, she was sure of that. Pat had always been able to read her like a book, but today even a stranger would be able to see that Marianne was visibly upset; her face was flushed, her eyes were glassy, and her hands were trembling.

"The only thing that's wrong," Marianne insisted, pulling away from her mother, "is that I'm late. I don't want to keep Chris waiting." She pulled a light jacket out of the hall closet, shrugged into it, and opened the door. "I'll be back later," she threw over her shoulder as she escaped.

Pat heard the door close behind her with a sharp click. There had to be more than just the prospect of tardiness to make Marianne leave in such an abrupt fashion. She briefly wondered if it was something to worry about, then dismissed it, knowing how teenagers tend to overreact to the slightest things.

Marianne had always felt that the elevator ride up to Chris's office was a long one, but it had never seemed so interminable as it did that day. The car seemed to stop at every floor before it reached the penthouse that served as the architectural offices of Frame Enterprises.

She stepped out, and in her haste, never even bothered to announce herself to the receptionist. She practically ran down the hall until she reached his desk.

Chris Peterson was an architectural apprentice. His job wasn't important enough to merit his own office, so he shared space with several other apprentices. They all looked up when she entered.

"Chris," she blurted out. "I have to talk to you. In private."

"What is it?" he asked, annoyed. The project he was working on had a tight deadline and the last thing he needed was an interruption.

Marianne said nothing. She turned on her heel and went into the hallway, assuming that he would follow.

He did. Running a hand through his curly dark hair he parked himself in front of her. "Is something wrong?"

"Chris, I'm pregnant," Marianne whispered. People bustled by in the hall but were moving too fast to be able to catch their conversation.

She watched as his brown eyes widened and then returned to normal. His face, a handsome one with a strong nose and wide mouth, became noncommittal.

"Aren't you going to say anything?" she pleaded. She had known he wasn't going to greet the news with joy, but she had been hoping for some sympathy for her predicament. After all, it was his predicament, too.

"What can I say?" he answered evasively. "You're sure?"

"The test was positive. The doctor called this morning," she told him. "What are we going to do?"

He shrugged. "What do you want to do?"

She leaned against the wall and put a hand up to her flushed face, wishing she could cool it with a touch. Chris had been so ardent when they'd made love; why was he being so impassive now? She pulled herself together and broached what was on her mind. "I want to get married. We've talked about it, haven't we?"

Chris groaned. "We've talked about marriage, yes, but we haven't talked about marriage and a baby. Marianne, I'm not ready for that. I can barely support myself on my salary here."

"I can get a job," she offered, desperate to make the plan seem feasible. "If we both work we could manage it."

"How are you going to work and take care of a baby?" he challenged.

"There has to be a way," she insisted.

"I don't see how—" he began, but she cut him off.

"We'll find a way. Chris, I love you," she implored. "That's all that matters, isn't it?"

He laughed derisively. "In books that's all that matters. But life isn't like books. This isn't a fairy tale."

Marianne felt a chill course down her back. "Do you expect me to give up our baby?" Was that what he wasn't saying? "Do you want me to go away somewhere, have it, and then put it up for adoption? I can't do that."

"There are other ways. . . ." he suggested. "You don't have to have it." His eyes met hers in a cool confrontation. "You know what I mean."

She gasped. "No, I could never do that." She couldn't believe what he was suggesting: an abortion!

"Lots of women do, Marianne, and

then they go on with their lives. You're not any more ready for a child than I am. Be sensible."

"Be sensible!" She fought to keep the tears from springing to her eyes. "After all we've meant to each other? I thought you loved me. How could you suggest such a thing?"

"I do love you," he whispered, pulling her closer to the wall as someone tried to edge around them. "But mistakes happen. We can't let them ruin our lives."

"This isn't a mistake. You talk as if this were just a *thing* that's happened to us. It isn't a thing. It's a real human being. It's our child. You can't get rid of it because you think it's inconvenient. You say it might ruin our lives, but what about its life? Doesn't it have the right to live?" Her words spilled out in a vehement jumble. She hadn't thought she'd felt so strongly about this issue. She supposed a woman never did until she was personally confronted with it.

"Calm down," he instructed, looking around nervously. "Do you want everyone to know?" He patted her on the shoulder off-handedly, as if she were a child who needed settling down. "Look, you're in no shape to make any decisions right now."

But she was too upset to listen. "I've made my decision. I want to get married."

Ever since she'd arrived at his office she'd sensed that he was withdrawing from her. How could he do that? Hadn't he told her, over and over again, how much he loved her? "I want to get married," she repeated stubbornly, as she saw him staring off into space, looking as if he wished she'd disappear.

At first, his face hardened and she noticed his fists clenched into angry balls. And then, as if some sudden change had occurred within him, his look softened. He smiled at her. "All right, Marianne, if that's what you want."

Her heart leaped in her chest. "We'll get married?" she asked excitedly.

"Sure, why not?" He was all smiles and charm now, like the Chris of old.

It wasn't exactly the way she'd envisioned a marriage proposal, but under the present circumstances Marianne figured it was the best that could be done. She brushed aside a tear and returned his smile, stepping forward for the hug she'd assumed was waiting. But he didn't offer it. Her smile wavered.

"I don't want you to tell anyone. Not yet," he instructed. "Let's keep it to ourselves."

"But why?" she implored. An engagement was one of the happiest events in a woman's life. Being able to tell her family and friends would help to ease the fear she felt when she thought about becoming a mother. To keep their engagement a secret would be torture.

"When we set the date, we'll tell everyone," he assured her.

"Let's set it now, then." There was no reason not to.

"Marianne, I have half a dozen people breathing down my neck for these plans I'm working on," he explained, suddenly cross. "We can do it tomorrow."

"Tomorrow? Won't I be seeing you tonight?"

"I'll be working most of the night." He began to edge toward the door to his office. "In fact, I should be working right now."

Meekly, Marianne let him go. "Call me tonight?" she pleaded.

"If I have the time," he answered, and then he disappeared into his office.

In a dazed state of mind, Marianne wandered down the hallway to the elevators. She was going to be married. But she couldn't tell anyone. She was going to have a baby. But she couldn't tell anyone that, either. She felt as if she were floating in limbo, her life out of control.

But that wasn't true, was it? She reminded herself to look on the bright side of things as her mother had always told her to do. As she waited for the elevator she decided to count her blessings. Yes, she was going to be married. In a few weeks she'd be Mrs. Chris Peterson. And, yes, she was going to have a child, his child.

She imagined a boy with Chris's good looks, and a wave of optimism flooded through her as she stepped through the elevator doors. It was all going to happen. And everything was going to turn out fine.

Marianne returned home later that afternoon in high spirits, a tiny package secreted beneath her jacket. She'd spent an hour or so in a baby boutique not far from Frame Enterprises. She'd gone there on a whim, thinking she'd just window-shop, but the window display had drawn her in and she'd been trapped, exclaiming in awe over all the darling little things.

Striking up a conversation with another woman, she'd learned what she'd have to buy to prepare for the little one's arrival. She looked at kimonos and gowns and sleepers and diaper covers and little two-piece sacque sets. She priced a crib and sheets and bumper pads, a wind-up swing, a high chair, and an enormous stuffed giraffe that probably cost as much as a week of Chris's salary.

And then she hadn't been able to stop herself from buying something right then and there: a sweater with hat and booties to match, decorated with a parade of ducklings following their mother. The set was in yellow, which the saleswoman assured her was appropriate for either a girl or a boy. She'd had it gift-wrapped, her first present to the baby.

With a smile on her face, she removed her jacket with one hand, clutching the gaily wrapped box in the other. When she heard her mother enter the living room from the kitchen, she quickly stowed the package in the back of the hall closet. Then she casually hung her jacket on a hanger, sure that her mother was far enough into the living room to be able to spot her around the banister of the stairs.

"Hi, Mom," she chirped brightly and joined her mother on the couch.

Pat couldn't understand how Marianne could leave the house practically crying, and then return looking as if she were on top of the world. What had happened in between? "Did you have a nice lunch, dear?"

With a start, Marianne realized she hadn't had any lunch at all. She'd have to sneak into the kitchen at some point and fix a sandwich. Dinner was hours away and she was unaccountably ravenous. But then she smiled. Of course she was hungry. She was supposed to be eating for two now.

"You're smiling," Pat observed when she didn't receive a verbal answer. "You must have had a nice lunch."

"Hmm," she murmured. She was wondering if eating for two meant eating twice as much. She thought of twice as many hot fudge sundaes and twice as many hunks of her mother's chocolate cake and realized that pregnancy definitely had its good points.

"Marianne!" Pat chided. "Are you there?"

Her mother's voice brought her back to reality. "Oh, yes, I'm here."

Pat shook her head. "Are you all right?"

"Of course I am. Why?"

"Well, this morning you looked as if you'd been crying. Now you look happier than I've seen you in months. What's going on?"

Marianne knew her mother would persist until she found something out. Although she'd promised Chris to keep their upcoming marriage and baby a secret, she was bursting to tell someone her good news, especially her mother. But she'd rather tell her mother that she and Chris were going to be married than that she was soon to be a grandmother. Besides, if she broke the news of their engagement first, it would make telling her about her pregnancy easier afterward. That way, events would seem to follow as they normally did, even though her mother would put two and two together immediately.

"Mom," she said, turning to her happily. "Chris and I are engaged."

Pat averted her eyes to Marianne's ring finger and then raised her eyebrows.

Marianne giggled nervously. "Not officially." How like her mother to be aware of all the proprieties.

"That's wonderful, Marianne." Pat feigned pleasure. "But Chris will have to talk to your father. That's usually how it's done, you know."

Marianne nodded and said, "Sure."

Pat's mind was racing, **and** she struggled to keep her emotions in check. "Are you certain it's wise? You haven't known him very long."

"Haven't you always told me that I'll know it when it's right?" Marianne challenged. She had hoped her mother would be happy for her, but she didn't seem that way.

"Yes," Pat agreed.

"Well, it's right." Marianne rose and wandered over to the living room window, where she fiddled with the drapes. "And it won't be a long engagement. We're going to get married right away."

Pat sighed audibly.

"Mom, I want you to be happy for me. I'm terribly happy."

She wanted to believe her daughter, but she found it hard to. If Marianne was as happy as she claimed to be, then why had she been so upset this morning? It didn't make sense. "I am happy," she said, trying to disguise her trepidation. "I'm just surprised, that's all."

"So am I," Marianne replied. "But Chris is very impatient."

"Shall I tell your father to expect a visit from him tonight?" Pat thought she had better prepare John for the news. He liked Chris even less than she did.

"Not tonight," Marianne informed her. She hadn't even considered this when she'd broken the news to her mother. Knowing her father wouldn't be pleased about her marrying Chris, she had no idea how she was ever going to tell him about the baby. "He's working late. He didn't want me to tell anyone until we could do it together, but I couldn't resist spilling the beans to you."

Pat nodded slowly.

"And, Mom?"

She looked up.

"Don't tell Dad yet. Let's have it be a surprise," she suggested with a cheer she didn't really feel.

Pat nodded again. "Surprise" wasn't the only word for it.

"No way," Chris Peterson mumbled to himself as he stuffed the contents of his personal drawer in a cardboard box. It was late, past midnight, and he was alone in the offices of Frame Enterprises.

He'd finished the blueprint that everyone would be waiting for the next morning. Little did they know it was going to be his last. Chris Peterson was leaving town.

He'd meant it when he'd told Marianne he wasn't ready to be a father. How could he have known she'd been foolish enough not to have protected herself? It wasn't his fault, and he wasn't about to suffer the consequences. The only reason that he'd told Marianne he would marry her was to keep her from making a scene. He had no intention of being a husband, or a father, and he certainly wasn't going to let anyone push him into it.

After pulling on his coat and picking up the box, he flicked off the office light and left the room. He took the elevator downstairs to his car and threw the box into the back seat with the other cartons he'd just packed back at his apartment. It hadn't taken long to get all his things together. He was used to living meagerly since he'd always been on the move.

Starting the engine of his car, he swung out of the parking space and headed toward the highway. When he had to decide whether to go west or east, he chose west.

"Go west, young man," he muttered, then laughed. There would always be new towns filled with people who wouldn't care where he'd come from or what he'd done. Bay City had been one. And he would have no problem getting a job. His good looks and charm had always made up for his lack of experience.

That's right, he thought to himself, *there's always a new town. And new women.* With a smile on his face he thought of all the pretty young women he'd soon be meeting wherever it was he decided to settle. Accelerating, he crossed over into the fast lane and felt care slip away as he pushed the pedal to the floor.

"Good-bye, Bay City," he announced to no one but himself. "And good-bye, Marianne. Sorry it had to end this way."

But Chris Peterson didn't look sorry. In fact, by the time he reached the Bay City limits he had nothing to feel sorry for. He'd already forgotten all about Marianne Randolph.

Chapter Three
Past Intrigues

Iris Cory Carrington Delaney stood before the door to her father's house and rang the bell. In the reflection of the inset glass she caught a quick look at her face. Across its regal features she detected an expression of annoyance.

And why shouldn't she be annoyed? Why did she have to ring at her own father's home? She should be able to just sweep in and announce herself. But the Corys had a maid whose purpose it was to announce guests. Rachel had made that clear to her on the several times she *had* just swept in.

It rankled her that she had to ring. In truth, everything about her father's marriage to Rachel rankled her. She didn't

like to think that there was any other
woman in her father's life but herself.

She put a hand up to her hair and patted
its carefully coiffed curls. She had it done
every other day so that it was always
elegantly blond and styled in the most
up-to-the-minute fashion. Her nails were
taken care of at the same time because she
hated to have even the smallest chip in an
otherwise perfect manicure. Iris looked the
way she was: a rich, pampered, indulged
woman who was used to getting her own
way.

When the maid finally answered the
door after making Iris wait what, to her,
seemed an interminable amount of time,
she entered and relieved herself of her
coat, purse, and a pile of presents. Then
she followed the maid into the front parlor, where Mac and Rachel were chatting
on the couch.

"Iris!" Mac said with a welcoming smile.
"I was wondering when I'd get to see you.
We saw Robert yesterday. How was your
honeymoon?"

"Splendid," she said, and then turned to
his wife. "Hello, Rachel."

"Good morning, Iris," Rachel said.
"Would you like a cup of coffee? We've just
finished breakfast."

She shook her head. Rachel was always
polite to her, Iris had to admit that. It was
another one of the things about Rachel
that annoyed her. Smoothing the wool of

her impeccably tailored suit, she sat in a chair facing the couch.

"The cruise was marvelous," she continued. "Except for some dreary days when all it did was rain, we had sunshine and blue skies the whole trip."

"And now you're back. It's lovely to see you, dear."

Mac did seem genuinely glad to see her. And yet, there was something in his smile that was more than just gladness to see her, Iris thought. He looked happier than she'd ever seen him.

"I brought you some lovely presents that I left on the front hall table. I hope you like them."

"I'm sure we will," he said. "Now, how's that grandson of mine? He must have missed you terribly while you were gone."

"I missed Dennis, too," Iris said with a sigh, thinking of her son from her previous marriage. "But the nanny took wonderful care of him, and of course he's thrilled to have Robert for a father now."

"Yes," Mac replied, "every child should have a father."

A special look seemed to pass between Mac and Rachel, she noticed. As if they had some kind of secret that they were keeping from her. Never being one to care for exclusion, she plunged right in with a question, hoping to find out just what the secret was.

"You two look exceptionally happy,"

she drawled lazily to disguise her avid curiosity. "What's going on?"

Rachel caught Mac's eye and smiled. She had known it would be impossible not to tell Iris about her pregnancy, but she hadn't expected her to pick up on their secret so quickly. She had to hand it to Iris, not much slipped by her—especially where her father was concerned.

"Shall we tell her, Mac?" she asked playfully, half enjoying the uneasiness on Iris's face as she had to contemplate the prospect of *not* being told.

"Of course," Mac said, beaming.

Rachel gave her her nicest smile. "Iris, Mac and I are going to have a baby."

With grudging admiration Rachel watched her struggle with her emotions and then present a face so clear of distress she almost had to think that Iris meant what she said next.

"How wonderful!" She stood and approached her father and gave him a hug, but she could barely control the feelings that surged within her.

A baby! It was dreadful enough that her father had remarried. But now, to have another child . . . It was almost too painful to consider. She had been an only child and she would have preferred it to stay that way. Now there would be another claim on her father's attention. She could hardly stand it. Nor could she stand the happy look on Rachel's face. But she couldn't let her know how horrible this news was making her feel.

"Do you have a doctor, dear? Because if you don't I know a wonderful one who—"

Rachel cut her short. "I have a doctor, Iris, but thanks for your offer." How like her to want to meddle, she thought.

"Well," Mac said as he rose from the couch. "I hate to leave such lovely company, but I've got to get to the complex and take care of some things before I leave for Washington." He kissed his wife affectionately.

"You're going to Washington, D.C., Daddy?" Iris asked, a plot beginning to brew in her mind.

"Yes, I have to take care of some business." Now he came to Iris's side and gave her a quick peck. "But I'll be home in a few days."

Iris faked concern. "You're going to leave Rachel in her condition?"

Rachel laughed. "I'm not sick, I'm just pregnant."

Mac shook a playful finger at his daughter. "I'll expect you to take good care of her while I'm gone."

He had always tried to ignore Iris's obvious dislike of his wife. He found it hard to believe that the two women he loved best couldn't get along, and so he had always encouraged a friendship that neither woman really felt capable of.

"Of course, Daddy. Of course I will,"

she lied, then kissed her father good-bye. "Have a wonderful trip."

As Mac left, Iris resettled herself in the chair.

"I think I would like some coffee, after all," she said to Rachel, who accommodated her by pouring her a cup.

"Rachel," she began, after she was served, "I hope you won't think I'm interfering, but do you think it's a good idea to have a child? After all, Daddy is so much older than you are. Do you think it might be too much of a strain for him?"

Rachel had known that as soon as Mac left Iris would abandon her little show of happiness and try to burst the bubble of joy she felt whenever she thought of her baby. But this time, she was determined not to let Iris get under her skin.

"Mac has been wanting this baby for a long time, and so have I. It's not a strain for him, it's what he's been hoping for."

Quietly, Iris stirred the cream into her coffee. "And you don't mind his going to Washington? It's a long way from here."

"No, I don't mind. He'll be home in a matter of days." What was she getting at? Rachel wondered. She had learned to be suspicious when Iris became quiet like this. It was always the calm before the storm.

"I'm only thinking . . ." Iris paused for a dramatic effect. "Well, it's nothing, really." She went back to her stirring.

Rachel knew she would be better off not asking but curiosity got the better of her. "What is 'nothing really,' Iris?"

"Oh," she murmured as she set the spoon precisely next to the cup in her saucer, "only that Daddy once knew someone in Washington." With her face the picture of innocence, she gazed at Rachel. "But that was a long time ago, after all."

Rachel sighed. "All right, Iris, why don't you just get to whatever it is you want to tell me." She knew she was concocting some scheme designed to make her unhappy. She might as well know what it was before it happened. At least she would be prepared for the worst, then.

"This was before he knew you, of course." Iris couldn't resist twisting the knife a bit before she plunged it in.

"Of course," Rachel replied dryly.

"Her name is Tracey DeWitt. She's from a very old Washington family. We went to the same schools. In fact, that's how Daddy met her. She was a friend of mine."

"Do you mean to say that Mac was involved with her?" She couldn't imagine Iris encouraging a relationship between one of her friends and her father. It wasn't like Iris to encourage a relationship between *any* woman and her father.

"Quite," Iris answered simply, and as if she'd read Rachel's mind she continued, "Of course Tracey was very young for Daddy, but she was sophisticated and well bred. They made a lovely pair. I loved seeing them together."

And the Pope isn't Catholic, Rachel thought to herself sarcastically. Iris had probably disliked Tracey, *if* she had gotten involved with Mac, as much as she disliked Rachel. But she knew that wouldn't stop Iris from pretending that she approved of the relationship if she thought it would cause Rachel any discomfort.

"In fact, I think they would have married," Iris went on. "I don't know why they didn't. I only know that Daddy was heartbroken when Tracey broke things off."

Rachel didn't believe a word of it. "That's nice to know. But as you said, it was a long time ago, wasn't it?" She started to straighten some things on the coffee tray, hoping that Iris would sense that she considered their visit over and leave.

But Iris obviously wasn't finished. "Yes, it was a long time ago and I never would have brought it up," she said, suddenly deciding that a bold-faced lie would suit her purposes best, "but I just heard from Tracey the other day. She asked for Daddy. She wanted to know his telephone number at the complex." With a look of sly triumph she raised her eyes to Rachel's. "I gave it to her."

Involuntarily, Rachel's breath caught in her throat. She didn't want to believe one word of what Iris had just told her. She knew Iris was doing her best to make her think that her husband was deliberately going to another city to renew an affair with a woman he'd known before her.

Rachel knew Iris was lying. She had to be. Mac wasn't interested in any woman but herself; she knew that to be true, just as she knew it was true that the sun rose in the east and set in the west. She was that sure of Mac's love.

But Iris had planted a seed of doubt. And what woman isn't susceptible to doubt when she loves a man? Especially, Rachel thought, when the woman was herself. A sharp pain began to twist in her chest.

"Then perhaps Mac will get in touch with her when he gets to Washington," she finally said, mustering a brave front. "For old times' sake." She refused to let Iris know that she had said anything to upset her.

"Perhaps," Iris replied. "Daddy always has had a soft spot in his heart for the women he's loved."

That, Rachel wanted to say, *is the only bit of truth you've said all morning, Iris, because if he didn't have that soft spot, he would have disowned you a long time ago.*

"Well, I really must be going," Iris said and rose. "I have a million things to take care of now that Robert and I are back."

She swept out of the parlor and Rachel followed.

In the front hallway she pointed to a pile of gaily wrapped packages. "I hope you enjoy what I brought back for you," she said as she slipped into her coat.

"I'm sure I'll love it," Rachel said, happy to watch her prepare to leave.

"And I'll be back soon," she threw over her shoulder as the maid opened the door for her. "I intend to obey Daddy's wishes explicitly. While he's gone I'm going to take *very* good care of you, Rachel."

The door shut behind her.

Rachel dismissed the maid and then leaned against a chair in the foyer. As always, Iris's words had a double meaning. Her "good care," Rachel knew, had only just begun.

Rummaging through the bottom drawer of her writing desk, Iris impatiently pushed things aside. "Where is that dreary address book?"

Every year she made a new address book and kept the old ones stored away. When people moved and changed their numbers and addresses she hated to cross out the old and write in the new because it looked so messy, so she just transferred everything to a new book at the end of the year. Except, of course, for the people whose names were never transferred because their friendship had lapsed. That was the case with Tracey

DeWitt. Her friendship with Iris had ended as soon as she and Mac had become involved.

But now Iris was going to renew that old friendship. If she could find her number and if, she desperately hoped, she hadn't moved.

"At last," she exclaimed with relief. "Here it is."

Iris picked up the phone and, using a pencil to avoid chipping her nails, she dialed the number.

"Please be home, please," she pleaded as the connection was made and the phone began to ring.

"Hello?" a soft, well-modulated voice answered at the other end. The voice only suggested the lovely face it accompanied.

"Tracey?" Iris asked, although she knew right away who it was. "It's Iris."

"Iris? Iris Cory?"

"Yes, dear. How are you?" She knew that Tracey had to be wondering why she was calling. It had been quite a long time since they'd last spoken.

"I'm fine. And you?"

Iris could hear the reticence in her voice. "Just wonderful. But I'm Iris Delaney now. I've just recently married."

Why was Iris calling her? Tracey wondered at the other end of the line. It couldn't be just to tell her she was married. "Congratulations."

"And you," Iris began as if it were an innocent question, "are you married yet?"

Tracey laughed softly at the irony of it. "No, I'm still single. I guess Mr. Right hasn't come along."

Iris laughed, too, but there was a hard edge to it. "He will, dear. Just be patient."

"Where are you?" Tracey asked. It had always been hard to keep up with Iris, she remembered. She'd be in Europe one moment and then in New York or Palm Beach the next. Usually, though, she was only one step behind wherever her father was.

"I'm in Bay City now. It's a lovely town. So quiet, so picturesque. Such a lovely change from the social whirl." Iris paused for a moment, and then began in earnest to get to the point of her phone call. "And how is Washington? Still going to all the parties?"

"Some," she answered truthfully. "They begin to pall after a while. Always the same faces."

In truth, Tracey had begun to feel just a little trapped in Washington. She *was* always seeing the same faces, except now they were getting younger and younger. Society had a way of making an unmarried woman feel even older than she actually was. Tracey was barely into her thirties, only a few years younger than Iris, but she was beginning to seem antediluvian, even to herself.

"Yes," Iris agreed. "It can get so dreary."

Tracey had no reply. She was still wondering why on earth Iris had called.

"Someone I know was asking for you the other day, that's why I've called." Iris began to put the pieces into motion.

"Oh?"

"Yes. Daddy." Iris paused, waiting to see what Tracey would say.

"Mac?" Tracey exclaimed. What in the world could this be all about? Once, she and Mac had spent all their time together. He was an exciting companion. But gradually, so slowly that she had hardly been aware of it, he had called to see her less and less. At the time, she couldn't have helped but think that Iris had something to do with it because often, when she and Mac were together, Iris would call with some kind of problem that had to be taken care of immediately. And Iris had made no pretense of liking Tracey's involvement with her father. They had stopped being friends long before Mac had stopped calling. Tracey had loved Mac very much, but perhaps he hadn't loved her in the same way. At least that's what she had come to believe.

"Yes. He's coming to Washington. In fact, he's leaving today," Iris explained. "He asked me to get in touch with you. He'd like to see you when he gets there."

Why would Iris want to encourage a

relationship she had once fought so hard to destroy? Tracey wondered. Maybe she had judged Iris unfairly.

"Well, Iris, I don't know. . . ." The old feelings she had felt once for Mac began to well within her again. They were difficult to suppress.

Iris sensed her indecision and took matters into her own hands. She gave Tracey the name of the hotel at which Mac would be staying. It was the only one he ever stayed at in Washington.

"Why don't you get in touch with him?" she suggested.

"If I get the chance, I will, Iris." *Had* Iris come between them, Tracey wondered, and was she feeling guilty about it now and trying to make up for it by encouraging a reunion? But why wait so long? "I'll try," Tracey said. At this point, thinking about Mac and the good times they'd once shared, it would be hard not to call him.

"And, Tracey?" Iris said, thrilled that she had been so compliant. "It's lovely to speak to you again."

She hung up the phone before Tracey even had a chance to echo her sentiment.

To put the final touch on her plan, she picked up the phone again and dialed her father's number at the complex. Just in case Tracey didn't call Mac at his hotel she had to back up her plan by planting a similar idea in his head.

"Daddy," she said, as soon as Mac's secretary put him on the line, "you'll never guess who I just heard from!"

"Iris," he replied, just a touch of impatience audible in his voice. "I'm trying to wrap things up here before I go to Washington. Is this important?"

Iris pouted. "You know I wouldn't call unless it were. And, really, it has to do with Washington."

Mac sighed. There were a dozen letters that needed to be reviewed and signed and he still hadn't packed for a flight that was only a few hours away. "What is it?"

"Tracey DeWitt called this morning out of the clear blue sky. Isn't that a coincidence?"

Mac, signing letters as he spoke, wasn't really listening. "What coincidence?" It was lost on him.

"That you're going to Washington and that Tracey called," she declared with annoyance. "Daddy, are you listening?"

"Yes, dear, I am, but I'm in a rush you know." He put his pen down. "So, Tracey called you. I wonder why."

"Oh, just to chat mostly," she lied. "She's still in Washington."

"That's nice." He picked up his pen again and started signing letters. He wondered when she would get to the point of this infuriatingly interruptive phone call.

"Daddy, why don't you give her a call

when you're in Washington?" she suggested, realizing that her father's patience was beginning to wear thin. "I know she'd *love* to hear from you."

"I'll hardly have time. I've got meetings every minute that I'm there."

"Let me just give you her phone number, then," she said, pressing on.

"I don't think—" He began to object, but she was too quick for him.

"Write this number down. One evening when you have absolutely nothing to do but stare at the hotel room walls, you'll be glad you have it. It's 555-9532. Did you write it down?"

"Yes," he said with a sigh. There really was no stopping Iris when she got a bee in her bonnet about something. "I've got it." He folded the slip of paper and put it in his breast pocket. Maybe some night, for old times' sake, he would give Tracey a call. She had been an extraordinarily nice young woman, he had to concede.

"Good." Iris sighed with relief. Between the two of them, one would surely have to call the other sooner or later. "Now, Daddy, you have a wonderful trip."

"I will. Are you done with me now?" he teased.

She giggled. "Yes, I'm finished."

"Good-bye, then, love," he said gently and hung up.

Iris returned the receiver to its hook.

She had put the pieces into play. Now all she had to do was wait, and if the pieces didn't move the way she wanted them to, she'd just have to give them a nudge.

She leaned back in her chair and stretched her arms above her head with a luxurious shrug. Now that Robert was hers and Clarice had been taken care of, she didn't have to worry about that bit of business. She had all the time in the world to concentrate on making Rachel unhappy. And that was just what she intended to do.

Chapter Four
A Hasty Decision

Marianne put a gloved hand up to the door of Chris's apartment and tapped hesitantly. She had tried to get him at work several times this morning, but each time she'd called, the receptionist had said he wasn't in yet and had no idea when he would be. Was he sick? So sick he couldn't call the office to tell them?

She knocked harder when her first try brought no response. "Chris?" she called. Why didn't he answer?

She was about to start pounding when an older lady appeared in the hallway.

"If you're tryin' to get Chris Peterson, you're outta luck," she told her in a tired voice.

Marianne spun around to face her. "What?"

"He's gone. Left me a note with the key. Said he had to leave unexpectedly. Stiffed me for the rent, too," she complained. Obviously, she had been his landlady.

"That can't be!" Marianne exclaimed. "He's supposed to . . . I mean, we're supposed to . . ."

The woman handed her a slip of paper. "This his writing?" she barked.

Recognizing Chris's scrawl, Marianne nodded wordlessly.

"There you are," the woman said with a shrug. "Flown the coop."

How could this be happening? Marianne put a hand up to her head. It was beginning to throb. How could he have left town when he was supposed to be marrying her? Their conversation of the day before came back to her, and she recalled his initial reluctance then total acceptance of responsibility. Thoughts she couldn't bear to think began to surface but were cut off by the landlady.

"You one of his girlfriends?" the woman asked pointedly.

One of his girlfriends? Wasn't she the only one? Marianne's world had suddenly turned to sand and was crumbling all around her. She nodded, miserably.

"Ah, well," the lady said and patted her on the arm, noticing how distressed she was. "There's other fish in the sea." She gave her another half-hearted pat. "He was a nice lookin' one, though, nice look-in'," she mumbled as she trundled off down the hall.

"Wait!" Marianne called in desperation. "Did he leave an address? Somewhere he could be located?"

The woman laughed. "When they leave this quickly they usually don't. Forget about him," she advised. "That's the best way." She went back downstairs.

Forget about him? When she was carrying his baby? Tears began to stream down Marianne's face. What was she supposed to do now? Who could she turn to?

Feeling as if her legs had turned to cement, she forced herself to leave the building and get back into her car. She wiped her face with the back of her hand, and then leaned her fevered cheek on the steering wheel.

She'd visit her brother. Michael would know what to do. He always did.

Michael Randolph leaned forward and clasped his sister's hand. "I'm sorry, Mari-anne. I'm so sorry."

She had arrived at his apartment just as he was about to leave for one of his classes at Bay State. He'd left home when he'd started school this past fall. Marianne would have done the same except she'd postponed starting college. When it came time to register all she'd been able to think about was Chris Peterson. The idea of sitting through what she could only imagine as a lot of boring classes had paled in comparison to spending time with Chris.

When Michael saw the look on his twin sister's face—a look of such desperation and abandonment—he decided that he'd have to skip class today. His sister needed him more than he needed Bio 101. Now, after hearing her story, he realized that he probably wouldn't make any of his classes.

"What am I going to do, Michael?" she pleaded, her eyes red from crying.

He sighed. He'd never liked Chris Peterson. He'd seemed too slick, too sure of himself. And Michael also had known some things. . . . Well, he'd decided to give the guy a break, but now he regretted it more than he'd ever regretted anything before in his life.

Marianne kept her eyes on her brother, hoping he'd have some kind of answer. Although he'd been born only several minutes before her he'd always acted as a much older brother. Michael had inherited his father's seriousness, as well as his dark good looks. Even as children he'd always seemed wiser than his years.

Michael didn't know what to say, the problem just as overwhelming to him as it was to her. When the doorbell of his apartment rang he was ashamed to admit he was glad for the interruption. He hated to think that he'd disappoint Marianne by not knowing what to do. She'd always looked up to him.

"Glenda," he exclaimed when he opened the door and saw his girlfriend standing there. "Please come in."

"Why so formal?" she chided him, stepping into the room. She gasped when she saw his sister's tear-streaked face. "Marianne, what's wrong?"

Marianne looked up at her and began to cry again. "Oh, Glenda, I'm so glad you're here."

Michael had met Glenda on the first day of classes at Bay State and they'd soon become inseparable. She was a slim young woman with a coppery head of hair. Always full of fun and good spirits, she made everyone who knew her feel happy themselves. She was also sincere, compassionate, and giving.

Her heart went out to Marianne as she sat next to her on the couch. "Here." She offered her a tissue, which she had pulled out of her purse. "Blow," she ordered.

Marianne did as she was told.

"Michael, get her a glass of cold water," she commanded, and when he returned with it she handed it to Marianne. "Drink this. At least half."

She drank a quarter of it and was surprised at how much better she felt. She put the glass down.

"Now tell me what's the problem," Glenda suggested when it was clear that Marianne had regained control of her emotions.

"It's Chris Peterson," she whispered. "He . . . I'm . . ." She began to cry again.

Michael sat on the other side of his sister and wrapped an arm around her. "She's pregnant," he murmured to Glenda, "and Chris has left town."

Glenda looked up at him and he returned her knowing glance.

"Why are you looking at each other like that?" Marianne asked, confused. "Do you know something that I don't?"

Glenda sighed and stroked Marianne's hair. "The same thing happened to me. With Chris."

"But . . ." Marianne looked even more confused, and then turned to her brother. "You didn't tell me?"

"I would have, but I didn't think it would have made any difference." He wanted to be sure his sister knew it wasn't for lack of caring that he hadn't told her. "You were so in love with him, I just hoped he'd changed, or that you'd change him. I could kill myself now," Michael said angrily. "I wish the guy were still around. I'd kill *him*."

"Michael!" Glenda warned. Things were bad enough without his threatening to kill people. "That won't solve the problem."

"I guess you're right, Michael," his sister admitted thoughtfully. "It wouldn't have mattered what I knew about Chris." She mulled that over for a moment, then turned to Glenda. "What did you do when this happened to you?" she asked. "What did he say?"

She shrugged. "He refused to accept that it was his baby, insisting it couldn't be his. He had no reason to suspect it wasn't his, he just didn't want the responsibility."

Marianne nodded mutely. This sounded so familiar.

Glenda continued. "He said he wasn't ready to be a father." She laughed ruefully. "That was probably the only true thing he ever said to me."

"Did you have the baby?" Marianne asked. "Did you give it up for adoption?"

She shook her head. "I wasn't any more ready than Chris was to have a child. I had an abortion."

Marianne's eyes widened.

"I know it sounds like a horrible thing to do. I still think about the baby and wonder if I did the right thing, but I felt as if I had no other choice. I wondered if it was right to bring a baby into the world without a father, or rather, with a father who didn't care about it. And I wondered if I was strong enough to be a single parent and fight people's perceptions of me because I was a woman without a husband. People can be very cruel."

Marianne nodded slowly. She hadn't yet thought about any of this.

"I can't tell you what to do, Marianne," Glenda sympathized. "I can only tell you what I did. Someday I hope I will have a child." She smiled at Michael, who returned her smile. "And a husband who'll love me and the baby. That way our child will have the kind of start it needs to get by in this world. It's not easy even under the best of circumstances."

"Where did you go?" Marianne asked, "to have the . . ." She found she couldn't say it. "To have the . . . operation?"

"I went to New York. That's where I'm from. I stayed with my parents for a week."

"Your parents knew?" Marianne caught Michael's eye. She knew he'd feel the same way she did about their parents' knowing. It would be impossible to tell them.

Glenda nodded. "They're a little more open-minded than most parents. They sympathized with me and they've always believed in letting me make my own decisions. Once I had decided to have the abortion they supported my decision."

"My parents will never do that. Never," Marianne insisted. "I can't tell them."

Michael turned to his sister. "You're

going to have to tell them, sis. They'll have to know."

"But why?" she protested.

"Because they've always expected us to be honest with them. And they've always let us know that when we have a problem they're there for us."

"But this kind of problem?" she questioned in a strangled voice. "It isn't like I just failed a test or something. And they never liked Chris. They're just going to say, 'I told you so.'"

"Marianne, they'd never say that," he protested.

She began to cry again. "They're going to think I'm bad. They're going to be so disappointed in me. I don't think I can stand that."

"Can you stand lying to them?" he asked, quietly but firmly.

Marianne's tears stopped. "I don't think so," she replied in a quavering voice. "I don't think I can do that, either."

"Then you'll have to tell them," he reasoned.

"But what about Dad?" she ventured, the tears starting again. "He's always had such high hopes for me. This will kill him."

"Marianne," Glenda interjected gently, "it's not like you've done something that hasn't happened to lots of other women. You loved Chris, just as I did, and he took advantage of your love. You haven't done anything bad. You just loved the wrong man and let your heart rule your head. It can happen to anyone. It happened to me," she reminded her softly.

"I guess it did," Marianne said slowly. "Oh, why did I ever get involved with him?"

Smiling softly, Glenda put an arm around her. "I've asked myself that question a number of times. I still ask myself every once in a while. But wishing you can change the past never does you any good. You just have to deal with the matter at hand, and then go on with your life."

"But it hurts so much!" Marianne cried, ineffectually brushing with the side of her hand at tears that were now streaming down her face. It was impossible to stop them from flowing.

"It will hurt less every day," Glenda assured her. "And one day you won't think of it anymore." She handed Marianne another tissue and then the glass of water. "Here, finish this."

Marianne wiped her eyes and took several more sips of water.

"Better?" Glenda asked.

Marianne nodded.

Michael had been thinking about Marianne's situation while she talked to Glenda and had come to some conclusions about what he thought she should do. He stood up and began to pace. "Look, sis," he began. "If you decide you don't want to have the baby I'll support your decision. I promise I'll help you in whatever way I can. But," he remonstrated, "you have to promise to tell Mom and Dad."

She opened her mouth to protest.

"At least tell Mom," he pleaded. "She'll want to help too, you know, and she can also help figure out how to break the news to Dad."

Turning her eyes up to her brother, she saw that stubborn look she knew so well. He was right, of course. Her parents had to be told.

"All right," she conceded. "I'll tell Mom."

"Today?" he coaxed.

"Today," Marianne agreed. "I'll tell her when I get home."

She only hoped she had the courage to do as she said. It was going to be the hardest thing she had ever done in her whole life.

It was even harder than she'd thought it was going to be. When she returned home her mother was sitting in the living room having tea and looking through a magazine filled with pictures of brides.

"Marianne," she called when she entered the living room. "Look at this gown. Isn't it lovely?" She looked so excited and full of life. "Wouldn't you like something like this for your wedding?"

Marianne's heart sank. Quietly, she sat in the chair across from her mother. She had hoped there was going to be some kind of way to gently ease into what she had to tell her mother, but she could see that that was impossible. She took a deep breath.

"Mother," she began, "there isn't going to be a wedding."

The magazine dropped into Pat's lap. "No wedding?" she cried. "But . . ."

Marianne told her mother just what she had told her brother, only this time without tears. First she said that Chris had left town, and that he was gone for good. Finally she told her mother that she was pregnant and considering having an abortion. She was surprised at how calmly she was able to relate the news.

She wasn't surprised when the expression on her mother's face turned from shock to disappointment. But she couldn't understand the look of horror her mother assumed when she mentioned the abortion.

"No!" Pat cried. "You can't do that!"

"I don't know if I have any other choice," Marianne replied, her voice dead of emotion.

"You have lots of choices!" she exclaimed. "You can put the baby up for adoption, for one."

"I'm not going to bring a baby into this world and then abandon it," Marianne insisted with more firmness than she really felt. She had hoped her mother was going to be more sympathetic to her plight. But it seemed as if she had her own ideas as to what should be done.

"Well, then, we'll tell your father what Chris has done, and we'll find him and make him marry you. He can't do this to you."

"He already has done this to me, Mom. And besides, there's no way we can find Chris. He's gone."

"We'll get a private detective," Pat insisted, distraught. "Your father—"

"I don't want Dad to know," Marianne interrupted, her voice as hard as steel. If her mother's reaction was this severe, her father's could only be worse.

"Marianne!" her mother wailed.

"I don't want him to know. I don't want you tracking Chris down. Why would I want to marry a man who doesn't want me?" Marianne was shocked at the strength she was beginning to feel welling within her. "It's my life and I have to do what's best."

"But an abortion isn't the answer," Pat said and stood up to pace the living room floor. "They're not safe. Don't you know that?" she implored vehemently. "You can . . . you can . . . ruin your whole life!"

Marianne had expected her mother to be upset, but she hadn't expected such a tirade. She had never known her mother to be this distraught about anything. She hadn't known her views were this strong on this issue. What was there about it that made her so angry?

"My life is already practically ruined," Marianne said softly. "I don't see how an abortion will ruin it any more." She found it less difficult to say that word now.

"I want you to talk to your father about this, Marianne," her mother said with fire in her eyes. "He'll tell you, just as I'm telling you, that an abortion is out of the question."

"I am not going to talk to Dad about it and if you try to force me, I'll run away."

"Marianne . . ." her mother began in a warning tone of voice.

"I mean it. I'll leave Bay City and you'll never see me again."

"How can I keep something like this a secret from him?" Pat pleaded. "He'll know something's wrong."

"Not if you pretend there's nothing wrong," Marianne suggested.

"How can I do that?"

"You'll have to try," Marianne begged. "For me, Mom." She turned a pleading face to her mother. "Please."

Pat knew she couldn't refuse her daughter's plea. "He's going to have to find out," she said, knowing that she was going to concede to her daughter's wishes, "sooner or later."

"I'd rather it was later," Marianne admitted. "I just can't think about telling Dad right now. It was hard enough telling you." She began to cry.

Pat felt the tears welling in her eyes, too. Wrapping an arm around her daughter, she pulled her close.

"I'm so glad you did, darling," she murmured, brushing a lock of hair away from Marianne's forehead. "Don't worry, we'll figure this out. I promise you." She began to rock Marianne in her arms to soothe her sobs. "You have some cousins in Somerset; you could always stay with them."

Marianne, lulled by her mother's rocking, was too tired to protest. "Yes, I guess I could," she agreed.

"And you don't have to give up the baby," Pat continued. "We could raise it here."

Her mother's voice was soft and convincing, so convincing that Marianne began to imagine the child growing up in the house where she'd grown up, playing in the same yard and going to parties with the children of the friends she'd grown up with. It was a very pretty dream until she got to the end of it. Bay City was still, in many ways, a small, conservative town. She doubted that her child, her illegitimate child, would be invited to many parties, even if it were a Randolph.

Would her child be ostracized and pointed at and laughed at because it didn't have a father? Marianne thought it would. Would her child have to suffer for her own stupid mistake? Yes, probably so. Was it right to bring a child into the world knowing it would suffer? Marianne was beginning to think not.

"It will be my first grandchild," Pat murmured, interrupting her daughter's thoughts.

Wearily, Marianne let her mother continue her rocking. She wished that she could be as optimistic as her mother was about her future, but she couldn't. She didn't see any other option but to have the abortion. But for her mother's sake she would pretend to consider all options, and when the time came, she would do as she'd already decided.

What Marianne didn't know was that her mother was no more optimistic about her future than she was. Pat didn't really see how keeping the baby was going to be beneficial for anyone involved, and as for giving it up, well, that would probably be one of the most painful things Marianne would ever have to do in her life. But an abortion . . . She sighed and shook her head. It was absolutely out of the question.

"Don't worry, my darling," she whispered to Marianne, pulling her even closer. "Everything will be all right."

Marianne echoed her sigh, deciding to believe her mother at least for the moment.

Chapter Five
A Vow of Secrecy

"Rachel, hon, how about some coffee?"

Ada McGowan had just entered the Cory parlor, where her daughter was curled on the couch, gazing out at the view through the French doors at the end of the room.

Rachel uncurled her legs and stretched. "No more coffee for me, Mom. You know it's not good for the baby." She gave her mother a radiant smile and patted her belly.

"Of course," Ada said with a grin, "how could I forget the well-being of my newest little grandchild." She was just as happy about the news of the baby as Rachel and Mac were.

"Where's Jamie?" Rachel asked as her mother sat down next to her.

"In the kitchen with Nancy getting into trouble, I suppose. But don't worry. Beatrice said she'll keep an eye on them," she said, referring to the Corys' cook.

Ada usually came by in the morning to see her daughter and check up on her news. Nancy, Rachel's little sister, loved to play with Jamie and treated him like an older brother even though, in truth, he was her nephew. It always made Ada laugh to think that having a baby so late in her life had made such a relationship possible. She had never thought that she and her daughter would be raising their children together!

"How are you feeling this morning, by the way?"

"Fine," Rachel replied, patting her mother on the arm affectionately. "I'm a little queasy, but it usually goes away by noon.

Ada frowned.

"And stop your worrying," Rachel reprimanded. "It's perfectly natural."

"If you say so," Ada said with a sigh.

Rachel had to smile. Her mother worried about her; she had always worried about her; she would probably never stop worrying about her as long as she lived. It was just one of the side effects of being a mother, she mused, thinking of all the times she had worried about Jamie, and even now, worried about the tiny little being she was carrying inside of herself.

She was just about to remark on that to her mother when the doorbell rang.

Moments later the maid entered and announced, "Iris Delaney, Mrs. Cory."

Rachel and Ada shared a look that could only be said to approximate dread.

"Show her in," Rachel said, and then under her breath to her mother added, "It had been a nice day."

Ada gave her a wry smile. "I'll be in the kitchen visiting Beatrice if you need me."

"Thanks, Mom," Rachel said, awaiting Iris's entrance.

She swept into the room leaving a waft of expensive perfume in her wake. "Rachel dear," she exclaimed as she sank into the chair next to her. "I'm just checking up. I promised Daddy I would, you know."

Rachel tried to smile but had a hard time making her lips form a look of happiness at seeing Iris. After yesterday's conversation, she wondered what Iris had to say today. Probably more of the same, she realized wearily.

"Have you heard from Daddy?" Iris asked, helping herself to some coffee from the tray.

"He's only been gone since yesterday afternoon, Iris." Her questions seemed innocent enough, Rachel thought, but then Iris had only just arrived.

"He must be very busy." Iris paused and sipped. "I do hope he gets in touch with

Tracey DeWitt," she said slyly. "She so wants to see him."

Rachel rolled her eyes. "Iris, if you've come here to talk about Tracey again, I think you'd better change the subject."

"Does it bother you?" she asked with wide-open eyes. "I had no idea." Inside, she congratulated herself at irking Rachel. So her plan had been a success!

"It's not that it bothers me, Iris," Rachel said, refusing to voice her true feelings. "It's just that there are at least a dozen other things I'd rather talk about than one of Mac's old girlfriends."

Especially, she thought to herself, *one that's in the same city Mac is now visiting.* But she brushed the thought aside. She and Mac were happy. They were always going to be happy. Wasn't the baby she was carrying proof of that?

Iris raised her eyebrows and said nothing.

"How are you and Robert settling into your new house?" Rachel asked to change the subject.

"Fine," Iris replied briefly. She brushed an imaginary piece of lint off her fitted blue wool dress and readjusted the hem over her knee. "I do hope Daddy wrote the phone number down correctly," she mused softly, as if she were speaking to herself.

Rachel's head shot up. "What phone number?"

"Tracey's, of course. I called him yesterday and gave it to him." *Got you on that one*, she thought triumphantly when she saw the look in Rachel's eyes. She seemed worried.

But Rachel didn't stay worried. Impatience took over. "If Mac wants to see Tracey, I doubt he'll need you to supply him with her phone number. He's a resourceful man." She was pleased to note that Iris looked slightly crestfallen, so she continued, "But I don't think it matters one way or the other to him whether or not he sees Tracey. He's gone to Washington for business, not for the social whirl." The only way to deal with her was to bully her back.

Iris shrugged her shoulders. "We'll see, won't we?" was all she said.

Not able to stand this game of cat and mouse any longer, Rachel decided to ask Iris to leave, and wasn't going to be polite about it. But the doorbell rang again, and Iris was spared.

"Clarice Hobson," the maid announced.

Rachel kept her face impassive even though she knew that a meeting between Iris and Clarice was bound to be full of tension. Poor Clarice, she thought, to have to run into Iris at her own friend's house.

Clarice entered, and when she saw Iris,

uttered a barely perceptible little cry. "I can come back later, Rachel," she said in a tiny voice. "You have a visitor."

"Oh, no, Clarice," Iris said expansively before Rachel even had a chance to say a word. "Please stay. I was just leaving."

She rose, as did Rachel to give Clarice a quick welcoming peck on the cheek. The two women stood together as if against a common enemy as Iris prepared to go.

Not bothering to hide her scrutiny, Iris swept her eyes up and down Clarice's body. The last time she had seen her, Clarice had been very pregnant. Now she looked thinner and tired. *If she had only taken my money,* Iris thought, pityingly. She wouldn't have to be working for a living, wearing herself out at that dreary little diner every day. She could have been in another city leading a comfortable life until she could meet another man. That was something Iris was sure Clarice could do. Her type of woman always met men.

"I'll be going," she said with a wave of her hand. "Take care, Rachel dear. Don't bother to see me to the door. I know my way out, of course." She turned to Clarice. "So nice to see you again, dear."

Clarice avoided her eyes. "Yes, thank you," was all she could say.

Iris left the room. But just as she was putting on her coat, she overheard Clarice's first words to Rachel and decided it would be worth her while to conceal herself in the hallway. What Clarice had to say definitely concerned her.

"Rachel, Robert's been to see me at the diner. He says Cory's his and he won't stop until he can prove it!" It all came out in a rush as she sank onto the couch.

Rachel sat beside her and held her hand. "I thought that might happen. He was here the day before yesterday and saw Cory. We couldn't help it."

"I know, I know," she moaned. "But what am I going to do?"

The two women looked at each other helplessly. After all, what *could* she do?

Ada entered the room from the door that led to the kitchen hallway. When she saw Clarice, her face lit up.

"Well," she said. "I see the company is improving."

"Mom," Rachel said. "Robert knows."

"He thinks he knows," Clarice corrected her. "I wouldn't tell him. He came to the diner yesterday and started accusing me of keeping Cory from him. He says Cory has to be his." She pulled at the worn strap of her handbag nervously. She hoped Rachel and Ada would be able to help her figure out what to do.

"Honey," Ada said, sitting on the other side of Clarice and putting a comforting arm around her shoulder, "Cory *is* his. Now tell us what happened."

"He came to the diner while I was working. He made such a fuss I had to bring him into the back hallway. He said he'd been here the other day and he'd seen Cory."

"That's true," Ada said. "I'd brought Cory for a visit."

"Did you say anything to him?" Clarice asked.

"You know I wouldn't," Ada replied. "But he asked who Cory belonged to and I couldn't lie. I told him Cory was yours." Ada decided to be truthful at the risk of upsetting her friend. "He's not a stupid man, Clarice, he can put two and two together. And Cory does look so much like him. You can't expect to keep this from him forever."

"But I don't want him to know," Clarice wailed. "I can't tell him."

Rachel and Ada glanced at each other questioningly. What was keeping Clarice from telling him?

"Why not?" Ada asked softly. "He's his father. He should know."

Iris, still secreted in the hallway, held her breath. She had vowed to ruin Clarice if she ever told a soul about her threats. Had she succeeded in scaring her enough so that she'd keep quiet?

"I just can't," Clarice replied. "I can't." She would never tell anyone about Iris's threats. She knew it wasn't beyond Iris's power to completely ruin her life if she did.

Iris let out her breath, relieved to hear

that Clarice wasn't mentioning their meeting several months ago. But when she next heard the direction of the conversation she tensed.

"But, Clarice," Rachel prodded, "don't you think Robert has a right to know? Cory's his own flesh and blood."

"Robert's married to someone else now," she answered sadly. "Why should he want a baby from someone he didn't love enough to marry?" Tears began to well in her eyes.

"That's just the point," Ada said. "If he knew, he'd feel responsible toward Cory. Look at you, you're worn out trying to support yourself and the baby. If Robert knew Cory was his I'm sure he'd want to help you."

"But I don't want his help," she insisted firmly.

"But you need it," Rachel reminded her.

"I have my pride," Clarice said, and lifted her chin. "Cory and I don't have much, but at least what we have is ours."

Rachel and Ada gave each other another look. Clarice was being unusually stubborn about this.

Ada sighed. "I can't tell you what to do, hon, but if I were you I'd tell Robert. He's Cory's father and he should know it, if only because it's the truth."

This gave Clarice pause. She was an

honest woman, not used to the lying she was having to do to keep her son's paternity a secret. She hated herself for lying, and yet she knew that if she didn't she'd be putting her future, and her child's, in jeopardy.

On the other side of the wall, Iris continued to listen, wondering if Clarice would crumble. Would Ada and Rachel be able to pressure her enough so that she would finally give in and tell Robert? What concerned her the most was whether or not the truth would affect her hold on Robert. He loved the idea of being Dennis's new father. How would he feel if he knew for certain that there was another boy, his own flesh and blood, that he was *really* father to? Iris didn't like the way this conversation was going.

"I agree with Mom," Rachel admitted. "I think you have to tell him. Not just for his good, but for your own good, too, Clarice. I can see the worry in your face. How much longer can you go on like this?"

"I don't know," she conceded. "Until he stops bothering me. If I keep denying that Cory is his, what can he do? Cory's birth certificate says his father is unknown."

She flushed as she remembered having to tell the hospital officials that she didn't know who Cory's father was. They had looked at her in pity, and she had felt cheap and awful having to pretend that she was the kind of woman who wouldn't know who had fathered her child. But she had been forced to do it to protect herself and the baby.

"I didn't know that," Rachel said softly and gave Clarice a hug. "That must have been hard."

She accepted the sympathetic hug, but then pulled away proudly. "But it doesn't really matter, does it? Cory's mine, he's my beautiful son, and I know who his father is even if the rest of the world doesn't."

"Robert should know," Ada repeated softly but firmly. She refused to budge on this issue.

"No," Clarice said, her tone implying that she wasn't going to change her mind either. "I will never tell him. He didn't care enough to know before Cory was born; why should I be obligated to tell him now?"

"You're punishing him, Clarice?" Rachel asked. "That doesn't sound like you."

It wasn't like her, Clarice had to admit silently. It wasn't like her at all to punish someone only because they were weak and susceptible to someone like Iris Carrington. But wasn't she weak too? Wasn't she susceptible to Iris and her threats?

She still loved Robert, and in a way she felt sorry for him because he had fallen so blindly for Iris and her fancy ways and beautiful clothes and the money that made it all possible. But she couldn't let Iris ruin her life, and Cory's, too. For Cory's sake, she would never tell Robert, even though her best instincts fought to do just the opposite.

She sighed. "I know you're only telling me this for my own good. But I have my reasons. I can't tell him and I have to ask you to never tell him either." She saw Rachel and her mother look at each other in resignation. "You promised," she reminded them. "You have to keep to your promise," she chided.

Reluctantly, Rachel and Ada nodded.

"All right, hon, if that's what you want," Ada said.

"Your secret's safe with us," Rachel told her. "We're your friends and we'll do as you ask."

Out in the hallway, Iris relaxed. It didn't sound as if Clarice was going to tell Rachel and Ada about their little confrontation. And it didn't sound like anyone was going to tell Robert that Cory was his son. But just to be sure, she decided to keep listening for a moment or so more.

"Clarice," Rachel said. "Would you like to stay for a while and then have lunch?"

"I'd love to," she sighed, "but I have to pick up Cory. I left him with a babysitter so I could talk to you. I didn't want him to see me this upset." She turned to Ada.

"Should I bring him here, or drop him off at your house? I have the afternoon shift at the diner today."

"Bring him here," she replied. "I'll be here for a while. Rachel needs looking after."

"Oh, Mom," her daughter complained good-naturedly.

"Are you sick, Rachel?" Clarice asked, concerned.

"Just a little queasy . . . in the mornings," she added with a smile, figuring Clarice would understand.

Her face lit up. "Are you . . . ?"

Rachel nodded, laughing.

"How wonderful! Now Cory will have someone to play with."

The three women began to discuss babies and pregnancies and all the things concerned with child rearing.

On the other side of the doorway, Iris quietly slipped into her coat and prepared to leave, satisfied that the situation with Clarice was well in hand. She had no need to listen to the rest of their dreary little chirpings about motherhood.

With a smile on her face, she sneaked out the door, pulling it after her softly. Now that she knew she had Clarice right where she wanted her, she had more pressing matters to attend to.

Chapter Six
A Widening Gap

Several days after his sister had announced her disturbing news, Michael Randolph was upstairs in his old bedroom looking through a bookcase for his high school algebra textbook. The first semester of calculus at Bay State was giving him problems and he thought it would be a good idea to brush up on his general math skills before the problems escalated into failure.

When he'd arrived a few minutes earlier, his mother had been preoccupied with dinner preparations, and he hadn't been able to say much to her except a quick hello. He was glad she didn't have the time to ask him what he knew about Marianne. He hated to think that he was involved in some kind of conspiracy to keep her secret from the rest of the family, although he was pretty sure by now Marianne had told their mother. But, his father . . . Michael dreaded his father's being told almost as much as Marianne did.

He heard the front door open and his father calling for his mother. She must have entered the living room because he could overhear their conversation.

"Dinner will be ready in half an hour," Pat said as she listlessly sank onto the living room couch. Ever since Marianne had told her about her predicament she hadn't been sleeping well. She had tossed and turned at night, trying to find a solution for her daughter, but none ever came.

"Wonderful!" John Randolph replied. "I'm starving."

Michael could hear pages rustling as his father settled into his easy chair to read the evening paper. It was comforting to know that even though he was living in a new place and making his own life, the days went on as usual in his old home. He concentrated on finding his book, and for the time being, forgot about his parents downstairs.

"I thought we might go to a movie tonight," John suggested to his wife. "There's a new movie by that director you like, playing at the Bay City Triplex. Let's go after dinner."

Pat sighed. "Not tonight, John. I'm too tired."

He put down his paper and observed her pale face. "Is something wrong?"

She shrugged.

"You're going to keep it to yourself?"

"What?"

"Whatever it is that's bothering you," John replied. "You've been in a fog for days."

Pat stirred uneasily on the couch, then picked up a magazine, thumbing through its pages lackadaisically. "It's nothing," she lied.

"'It's nothing,'" he mimicked sarcastically. "You toss and turn all night and tell me it's nothing. Is it me? Is it something I've done?"

Inwardly, she cringed. Having to keep Marianne's secret was taking a higher toll than she'd thought it would. She could hardly look him in the eye these days. And she knew that her fear of his discovering that she was keeping something from him made her seem diffident and uncaring. "It's nothing you've done," she assured him, too fervently. "It's the weather. It's been so rainy." She knew it was a weak excuse.

John knew, too. "And was it the rain that gave you a headache last night? And the night before?"

Pat reddened beneath his inquisitive gaze. "I just didn't want to, John," she replied angrily. "Why does it have to be anything more than that?"

"Because a woman doesn't turn off to her husband for no reason whatsoever. Either he's doing something wrong, or she's got something on her mind that she's not telling him," he retorted. "Now, tell me. Am I doing something wrong, or is there something you're not telling me?"

"You're badgering me!" she cried and collapsed into tears. How could she tell him that the reason she didn't want to sleep with him was no fault of his? He had always been an exciting lover. But how could she generate any interest in the act of making love when it just reminded her of their daughter's actions? And how could she want to be intimate with her husband when she was keeping such a disturbing secret from him?

John rose from his chair and came to his wife's side. "Pat, you know when we don't talk about the things that are bothering us it puts distance between us. And that distance estranges us from each other. I don't mean to badger you," he insisted, stroking her fine blond hair, "but I'm concerned. You seem so unhappy."

Michael had finally found his book and was heading down the stairs when he saw his mother crying and his father comforting her. He stopped on the stairs, not knowing what to do.

"It's nothing, John. It will pass," she replied in a tiny voice.

"You're not going to tell me?" His concern was turning back to anger now.

Pat raised her tear-streaked face to him and shook her head. "There's nothing to tell," she persisted in her lie. "It will pass."

Out of eyesight, Michael watched his father's face set in an expression of annoyance. And sadness.

"We've been through so much together, Pat," John began in a low voice, "good and bad. But we could have avoided most of the bad parts if we'd just been honest with each other. I thought we'd both learned that."

She turned a face full of pleading toward him.

"Don't look at me like that," he begged. "As if I am being unreasonable. I'm not. You're being unreasonable by not telling me what's bothering you." He rose and grabbed his jacket off the arm of the couch.

Softly, Michael returned to the head of the stairs. He didn't want his father to know he'd witnessed this confrontation.

"Are you going somewhere?" Pat asked, disturbed that he might be leaving, but almost relieved if it meant she wouldn't have to face any more of his questioning. "Dinner's almost ready."

"I'll pass on dinner tonight, Pat," he

answered as he pulled his suit jacket on. "I've lost my appetite."

"But . . ." She rose from the couch to follow him to the door. "Please don't go."

"I have work to do at the office. I'll order something there." He turned to her. "If I'm going to feel as if I'm all alone while I eat, I might as well *be* all alone." He opened the door and left.

Pat stood in the entrance hall wringing her hands. When she heard a rustle behind her, she looked up and saw Michael coming down the stairs with a book in his hand.

"Found it!" Michael declared triumphantly, hoping that if he acted completely ignorant of what just happened, his mother might be able to forget it more quickly.

"Michael, do you have a minute?" she asked softly.

His heart softened at his mother's obvious distress. "Sure, Mom. What is it?" As if he needed to ask.

"I'm sure you know about Marianne's—" Pat didn't know how to put it "—problem." She decided to be euphemistic.

Michael plopped into his father's chair and balanced his textbook on his leg, watching it teeter back and forth. "Yes, I know," he admitted. "I encouraged her to tell you." His mother had always disliked it when he and Marianne, like most twins, had kept secrets from her. He wanted to let her know that they'd grown up since then.

"Did you also encourage her to have an abortion?" His mother's face looked worn and tired and pained, as if she were living her daughter's life as well as her own.

"No. But we discussed all the options," he confessed.

"It's *not* an option," she said fervently. "I want you to convince her of that."

"I can't do that, Mom," he answered uneasily. He hated to disobey his mother, but he felt strongly about Marianne's rights. "It's her decision."

"She'll ruin her life," Pat cried, as if she knew for certain that that could be the only outcome.

"How do you know that?" Michael asked reasonably.

"She will," she said, evading his question. "You don't know what kind of damage an operation like that can do to a woman." She'd said more than she'd intended to and quickly amended her statement. "I've read horrible stories about women who've been to back-alley abortionists. They're butchers."

"It's not like that anymore," he protested.

"How do you know?" she challenged.

"I read magazines, too, Mom," he said,

flinging her own argument back at her. "It's a simple procedure." He changed his tack. "But that's not really the question here. We have to let Marianne make up her own mind about what she wants to do, and then we have to support her. She needs all our help."

"Even if I know she's doing the wrong thing?"

"You have to trust her, Mom. You have to trust that she'll do what's right for her."

Pat mulled that over for a few minutes, then shook her head. "She's too confused right now to know what's right for her."

"And you do?"

"I'm her mother, aren't I?" Pat snapped.

"Yes," Michael replied. "But you're not *her*."

"If you won't help me, then I'll have to try to persuade her again myself." Her voice was steely.

He opened his mouth, about to try once again to convince his mother to let Marianne make up her own mind, when he realized it was hopeless. He knew that his mother, when her children were concerned, was like a lioness guarding her cubs. She had always been fiercely protective. Even now, when the best thing for them to do would be to back off a little and let Marianne reach her own decision, he couldn't really expect her to change her ways. The set expression on her face was proof enough that she wouldn't.

He said nothing. Picking at the binding of his textbook, he waited for his mother to speak again.

She stared off into space for a moment or two and then murmured softly, almost to herself, "I never liked Chris Peterson."

"I'll agree with you on that, Mom," Michael conceded, reaching over to give his mother's arm a comforting rub. He loved his mother very much. He knew she had to be suffering from Marianne's problem even more than he was, almost as much as Marianne.

"There is something you have to help me with though, Michael," Pat said, "and I'm sure you feel the same way I do." She gave him a direct look.

He knew exactly what she meant. "Marianne has to tell Dad."

She nodded her head. "I don't know how much longer I can keep it from him."

Michael knew.

"And I don't want to be the one who tells him," she continued. "It would be easier for the both of them if Marianne told him herself. If he hears it from me—" she shook her head "—he'll be angry that she kept it a secret from him. Especially when he finds out that we all knew and he was the only one who didn't."

"I know, Mom. I've tried to convince her to tell him, but she's so afraid he'll get mad or think she's failed him." He shook his head in sorrow. "She's so terrified of disappointing him."

"He may feel all of those things," Pat agreed, "but it won't last long. And then he'll be her fiercest ally," she said with certainty.

"I'll talk to her again," he promised.

"Good." She patted his hand in gratitude. "And there's one other thing you can do for me," she said, making a smile tug at her lips. It would be best not to let her son see how devastated she was by all of this. For him, she would act happier than she really was.

Michael cocked his head.

"I have a roast beef dinner that's going to go to waste unless you help me out. Your father's having dinner at the office."

Michael acted, too. He acted as if it were just another one of those nights when his father had to work late. "You've got a deal. All I was looking forward to was a macaroni dinner from a box."

Pat rose and pulled him from the chair. "You don't really eat that, do you?" she chided him.

Laughing, Michael told her that he did, and then told her all the other shameful things he ate now that he was a student. He kept his mother laughing all through dinner, amazed at how easy it was to pretend that everything was exactly as it should be.

* * *

Unfortunately, as soon as Michael left his parents' home later that evening, it was just as easy to remember that things were far less than perfect. His mother had told him that Marianne spent more and more time away from home in order to avoid her father, so he knew that she was at a girlfriend's house. He drove over there in hopes of intercepting her before she left. Seeing strain on his mother's face and the tension in his parents' relationship, he had had no problem agreeing with his mother that Marianne had to tell their father about her pregnancy as soon as possible.

As he pulled up in front of Marianne's friend's house, he saw her walking down the sidewalk to her car parked in the driveway. Rolling down his window, he called her name, and when she recognized him, he motioned for her to get into his car.

"What are you doing here?" she asked.

"We have to talk," he replied curtly.

"Are you angry with me?" she questioned. If Michael was mad at her she didn't know what she'd do. The tears that were always, lately, just a second away from spouting began to well in her eyes.

Michael saw the wretched look on her face and his heart softened. "Please don't cry," he pleaded. "I can't stand it when you do."

"All right." She swallowed and then took several deep breaths.

"I just spent the evening with Mom," Michael began as he turned off the car, deciding they might as well talk here.

"Where was Dad?"

"He left. Look, Marianne, Mom doesn't know, but I overheard them arguing. Dad knows she's upset about something but she won't tell him what it is. You're putting her in an awful position by asking her not to tell Dad. She's asked me to try to persuade you to confide in him."

"You're turning against me?" Marianne asked. Her brother had always taken her side.

"No, *you're* turning against *us*," Michael argued. "You're upsetting the whole family by asking us to keep a secret from Dad."

"But how can I tell him?" Marianne wailed. "He'll hate me."

"He won't hate you," Michael disagreed patiently. "He'll be hurt, but it won't last long. And think of how much better you'll feel when it's all out in the open."

Marianne considered that. Keeping this secret was taking a toll on her, too. She felt bad enough about herself as it was without adding the lying she was having to do to keep her pregnancy from her father. "The only thing is, Michael," she began slowly, "if I tell him about my pregnancy, I'll have to tell him about the abortion, too. He'll never let me have it."

Michael hadn't considered that, but he knew she was right. His mother and father were probably of like mind on that issue. He sighed. "Mom also wanted me to persuade you not to do it," he admitted.

"Do you think I shouldn't?" she asked. She'd been talking about it all evening with her girlfriend, and all they could agree upon was that each one of the options had its own particular kind of pain.

"I told Mom that it was something you had to decide yourself and that she should respect you enough to know that you'll make the right decision. For you."

"She's totally against it." Marianne shook her head sadly. "She doesn't see it as an option at all."

"I know," he agreed. "I know abortion is a sensitive issue, but I don't understand why she's so inflexible about considering it."

"I'm not going to be able to tell her, if that's what I decide to do," Marianne said.

"You're saying that that's going to be *another* secret?" Michael asked impatiently.

"What am I supposed to do?" Marianne exploded. "You say it's my decision, then you imply that I have to tell Mom. But you know if I do tell her, she'll forbid it. She'd probably lock me in my room or send me away. You know how stubborn she is." She paused before continuing. "So if I do it your way it won't really be my decision, will it, Michael? It will be Mom's."

Michael's heart went out to his sister, who was trying so hard in the worst of circumstances to make the right decision, which would affect the rest of her life. But was there no way out of this situation that didn't involve duplicity and lying? "What am I supposed to do?" he finally asked. "I know it's your decision, and Mom should respect that. I think it's wrong of her to try to persuade you to do something you don't want to do. But you're both putting me in the middle and I don't like it. I don't like lying to Dad either."

"You're not lying," she insisted. "You're just not telling him."

"That's a very fine distinction, sis, which I'm sure will be lost on Dad once he finds out."

"Are you going to tell him?"

"No, but you are," he declared firmly. "Because every day you wait pushes Mom and Dad further apart."

Unable to bear the emotional burden any longer, Marianne burst into tears.

"Look," he said, ineffectually patting her arm. "I know this is an awful time for you. But don't you realize that by asking me and Mom to keep your problem a secret, you're causing problems for all of us? I can't look Dad in the eye when I see him, and Mom practically runs in the opposite direction whenever he's around. It's not right to estrange us from him, and that's just what you're doing by asking us to keep mum."

Marianne was still for a while, taking in what her brother had said. Michael was right; it wasn't fair of her to ask him and her mother to cover up for her mistake. She turned to him. "I'm sorry, Michael. You're right. I've been feeling so desperate and so unhappy I haven't been thinking of anyone but myself." She stopped and gave her brother a long look.

Michael cocked an eyebrow, waiting for her to continue.

"I'll tell him tomorrow," she said. "I won't make you lie any longer."

Chapter Seven
Women's Lies

Rachel and Jamie were just returning from an afternoon walk by the pond on the Cory grounds when she saw Mac's limousine in the drive.

"Your father's home, Jamie," she told the small boy excitedly.

Jamie took off for the house as fast as his legs would carry him.

Rachel smiled. She was as glad as her son to see Mac was finally home. Approaching the house, she briefly wondered if she should ask Mac about Tracey De-Witt, but then realized it would just make her seem suspicious.

Well, she thought to herself, *I'm not really suspicious . . . just curious.* But all her thoughts about Tracey DeWitt vanished into thin air when she saw Mac open the door and hold out his arms for a welcoming hug.

"It's so good to be home, especially with Christmas approaching. I missed you both." He patted Jamie on the head, and then patted Rachel's stomach for good measure. "And the littlest member of the family, too."

Rachel grinned. "I missed you." She wrapped an arm around his waist as they went inside. "It seemed as if you were gone for months."

"A few days does seem like an awfully long time when you're away from the people you love, doesn't it?" Mac steered them into the parlor where a tray of tea and sandwiches was waiting.

"Jamie, since you've already eaten lunch, how would you like a snack? There's some milk and cookies in the kitchen," Rachel told her son. "And I think they're Beatrice's chocolate chip ones that you like so much."

"Oh, boy," Jamie exclaimed, and then turned to Mac. "You won't go away again before I come back, will you?"

"Not on your life," Mac said as he gave him a hug. "I'm not going anywhere for quite a while."

"Okay," Jamie said happily and went off in search of cookies.

"Darling, it's wonderful to see you again," Mac said, accepting the cup of tea Rachel had poured. "I hate these trips. It's just go-go-go all day, and then business dinners that seem to last all night."

Rachel settled on the sofa with her cup of tea. Now that they were alone, she wondered if it was time to ask Mac about Tracey. As much as she'd like to just ignore Iris's needling she found it difficult not to bring up the subject. It was so pressing on her mind, and she wanted to be relieved of her doubts once and for all.

"Mac," she began as she stirred some cream into her tea, "did you hear from anyone while you were in Washington?"

He cocked an eyebrow. "Like who?"

"Um," she stalled. How was she supposed to bring this up discreetly? Perhaps there was no way. Maybe a direct question was the best way to handle it. That was Iris's method and it always seemed to work for her. "Like Tracey DeWitt?"

"How in the world would you know about Tracey?" he asked incredulously. He'd never mentioned her to Rachel. In fact, he'd hardly even thought of her since their relationship had ended.

Her eyes met his and she gave him a one-sided grin. "A little bird told me."

"Let me guess," he said, suddenly understanding. "It wouldn't be a little bird named Iris, would it?"

Rachel nodded.

"Yes, I heard from Tracey. Apparently Iris told her I was going to be in Washington and so she called. Just to be polite, I suppose."

"Oh," Rachel said with a sigh.

"You're frowning," he observed. He sat next to her on the couch. "Has Iris been bothering you about Tracey?"

"You know your daughter awfully well, don't you?" she replied. When he shrugged good-naturedly, she continued. "She came over the other day and told me all about your so-called wild affair with Tracey. I guess she thought it would upset me."

"And I can see that it did," he responded, putting his arms around her. "It wasn't that wild, my love. And it was a long time ago. Right now all I'm thinking about is you," he said as he gave her an affectionate kiss, "and the baby."

"I love you, Mac," Rachel whispered against his rough cheek. "I guess that means I worry about you, too."

"You have nothing to worry about as far as I'm concerned. I'm the faithful type, you know. I'm strictly a one-woman man." He chuckled and drew her closer. "But Iris is someone to worry about."

"I just wish she would accept me," Rachel mused. "I've tried my best to be kind to her."

"I know you have, Rachel, no one could have tried harder. But she has always been such a demanding person. I suppose if I had been home more often when she was growing up she wouldn't be so insecure about my love now. But her childhood was the time when I was away most, building my business. Now I wish it had been different," he said with a sigh.

Rachel sighed, too. She knew what it was like not to have enough of a father. Her own father had disappeared out of her life when she was just a little girl. It had left a gap in her life that she had only just begun to fill with Mac's love and the promise of a bright future.

Wrapped in his arms and content with her world, she felt particularly expansive. Maybe it was time to make a serious effort at making friends with Iris. "If there were only some way to get through to her," she wondered out loud.

He shook his head. "I don't know why she sees you as such a threat. She wouldn't act as she does if that weren't the way she felt. I can't understand why she doesn't realize that loving you doesn't lessen my love for her. No matter what happens, you never stop loving your children."

"Maybe I should just be honest with her. You know, Mac," she said with growing conviction, "I've never just come out and asked her why she dislikes me so. Maybe if I did, it would clear the air."

"Why, Rachel," he said softly, "you really do want to be friends with her."

She nodded slowly. "I think now that

ANOTHER WORLD

I'm having a baby I'm more sensitive to her
unhappiness. It made me think when you
said that you never stop loving your children. I know I'll always love Jamie and I'll
always love our baby. Perhaps if I tell her
what you've said and how you feel, she'll
understand, too."

"That's a sweet thought." He stroked
her hair.

"I think I'll stop by at her new house
soon with a little housewarming present.
Maybe I can talk to her then." She snuggled into his chest.

Quietly, they sat on the couch, watching the sun set through the trees.

"But there's one thing you haven't told
me, Mac," she murmured and then prodded him with a finger.

"What's that?" he asked, contentedly.

"Well, you told me what Tracey said to
you, but you didn't tell me what you said to
Tracey." She smiled at him devilishly.

He laughed out loud. "You don't let go,
do you?"

"Not where my man is concerned," she
replied firmly. "So what did you say?"

"I told her that I was a happily married
man," Mac replied, grinning. "And then I
told her that my wife was a very possessive
woman with a heck of a right hook."

"You didn't!" she exclaimed, tugging at
his hair playfully.

"No, I didn't," he admitted and settled
her back down into his arms.

"But I wish you had," she said softly. "Because it's true."

Mac laughed with delight and drew her close for a long, passionate kiss. "It *is* good to be home again, my love. It truly is."

The next morning, Robert Delaney was disappointed when he entered the Cory parlor to find only Mac and Rachel finishing their morning coffee. He had hoped that Ada might be there again with Cory.

Maybe she's in the kitchen with him, he wondered to himself. But he couldn't get there without anyone finding out. He'd just have to ask.

"Good morning, Robert. So nice to see my new son-in-law," Mac said cheerfully and offered him a cup of coffee.

Robert waved it aside with a smile. "Hello, Rachel," he said and nodded.

She had a hard time meeting his eyes, but she forced herself to, not wanting him to realize she knew all about his scene with Clarice the other day.

"How's Iris?" she asked to end the awkward silence. "I'm thinking of visiting her today."

He shook his head. "Not today. First there's the dressmaker, and then there's the beauty shop." He laughed ruefully. "For a woman who doesn't work, Iris is always busy."

Mac chuckled. "Iris has to keep herself beautiful, you know. Even though you're back from your cruise, I'm sure you don't want the honeymoon to be over yet," he joked.

"No, we wouldn't want that," he said, and then dismissed Iris completely from his mind. "Rachel, is your mother here?"

Rachel knew why he was asking. Ada took care of Cory during the day now that Clarice was back at work. "No, she's not," she answered innocently.

"Ada's home with Nancy and Cory," Mac said. "Stop by if you want to see her. I'm sure she'd love the company."

Mac wondered why Rachel had discreetly poked him in the ribs as he offered the invitation, and why Robert suddenly looked distinctly uncomfortable. But he didn't think about it long because he was already overdue at the office and had to leave.

"I hate to leave the *three* of you alone," he said as he gave Rachel a hug, "but I've got to go."

"The three of us?" Robert asked, his eyes crinkling in confusion.

"I thought Iris would have told you," Mac remarked. "I guess she didn't."

Robert shrugged his shoulders. "I've been so busy getting my business back into shape after being away for so long that I don't get home until late." He didn't bother to add that he and Iris didn't discuss much at all lately. They ate dinner, mostly in silence, and then Iris retired early while he brooded about Cory and Clarice alone in the study.

He was beginning to realize that his marriage to Iris wasn't the melding together of two lives that he'd hoped it would be. In fact, their lives were almost totally separate: Iris had her socializing during the day and her beauty sleep at night; he had a business that had practically gone under from his long absence and which needed constant attention until he got it back on its feet again. Their marriage was a lonely affair so far.

"Then let me tell you," Rachel said, interrupting his reverie. "Mac and I are going to have a baby."

"Oh!" His face lit up. "That's wonderful news." He pumped Mac's hand and kissed Rachel softly on the cheek. "Congratulations."

He stepped back from the happy couple and observed them, unable to keep the feeling of sadness that was welling within him from showing on his face. *This is how it should be,* he thought. *Two people happily looking forward to the birth of their child.*

"You look sad, my friend," Mac remarked.

"I was only thinking that I'd love to be in your place. But maybe I will be one day. I don't know how Iris feels, but I'd love to have a baby."

"Dennis would have a little brother or

sister and I'd be a grandfather again. That would be nice," Mac said with a wink.

Rachel didn't say anything. If she knew Iris at all, having another child was probably on the bottom of her list of priorities. She barely had time for Dennis, and Rachel couldn't imagine her getting up in the middle of the night to feed the baby. Somehow that just wasn't Iris's style.

"Well, you'll let me know," Mac said and gave Robert a pat on the back. "And now I really have to go." He kissed Rachel. "Bye, love. I'll try to get away early so we can go shopping for the tree."

"Okay, dear." After Mac left the room, she and Robert were alone and an uncomfortable silence began to brew.

"Rachel," Robert began as he sat next to her on the couch. "Can I ask you a question?"

She knew what it would be, but she couldn't deny his request. She nodded.

"I saw Cory Hobson the other day," Robert said uneasily.

"Yes, he's a lovely baby."

"Rachel, do you know who Cory's father is?" he blurted out.

She felt so sorry for this man who so desperately wanted an honest answer, but as much as she wanted to be truthful, she had promised Clarice never to reveal her secret. "His birth certificate says his father is unknown." At least that was as honest an answer as she could give. She rose and fiddled with some magazines on the coffee table.

Robert sensed her nervousness. "Why do I get the feeling that there's something you're not telling me," he said directly.

"I think Clarice is the only one who can answer your question, Robert." She put the magazines down and turned her back to him. "I can't."

"Clarice refuses to answer my question," he protested. "I was hoping you might. We're friends, aren't we?"

She turned to face him. "Yes, we're friends. But Clarice is my friend, too," she explained before she realized what an incriminating statement she had just made.

"There *is* something you're not telling me," Robert said, his voice rising angrily. "You know I'm Cory's father, don't you?"

"Robert, Clarice is the only one who knows who Cory's father is. For some reason she wants to keep it to herself. Why don't you respect her wish if that's what she wants?"

"Because, dammit, if I have a son I deserve to know. I want to be a father to him. I want to share in my child's life," he insisted.

"You said that you and Iris might have a child," Rachel reminded him, although she herself realized the improbability of that ever happening. "Have a child with

Iris and let Clarice lead her own life," she pleaded. "It's for the best."

He rose to his feet. "I can see that you're not going to tell me what I need to know."

"I'm sorry, Robert," she said sadly. "I really am."

"That's all right," he sighed wearily. "I'm sure she's sworn you to secrecy." He headed for the door. "You're a very good friend, Rachel, I only wish you were mine and not Clarice's." And with that he left the house.

Rachel sighed as she sat back down on the couch. The poor man. If only Clarice weren't so proud and stubborn. But Robert was married to Iris now, and perhaps Clarice's way of going about things actually was for the best. She supposed that time alone would tell.

"Louise, dear, would you answer that?" Iris trilled down the hallway from her bedroom. She was busy trying to decide what she should wear this morning: the red suit with its gold-braid edging or a lavender dress that so nicely played up her blond hair.

She chose the red suit since she had a new pair of heels she was dying to wear that would look wretched with the lavender. Satisfied with her decision, she was about to put the lavender dress away when Louise appeared at her doorway.

"It's Ms. DeWitt, madam," she announced, in her usual impassive way.

"Oh, good," she declared, her face lighting up at the thought of getting to hear how Tracey did with her father. "I'll take it in here," she said, dropping the dress back onto the bed.

Her servant nodded and left.

Picking up the phone, she waited until she heard Louise hang up the living room extension. She never liked to think that anyone might be listening to her conversations, even a servant.

"Tracey," she sang. "How are you, dear?"

"Fine, but a little puzzled."

"Oh?"

"Iris, I thought you said Mac wanted to speak with me."

"I did. He did, didn't he?" Iris lied.

"I hardly think so. He seemed surprised that I called. All he talked about was how very happily married he was and how he loved his wife."

"Of course that's what he said," Iris explained patiently as if Tracey had misunderstood Mac's intentions. "Men are always saying things like that on the telephone. They never tell you what they're really thinking."

"I think he meant it, Iris."

"I doubt it, dear. Weren't you able to have dinner with him?"

"He said he was too busy," Tracey replied. "He shut me down cold. It was rather embarrassing."

"That's Daddy," she said with a high-pitched giggle. "Always work before pleasure."

"I don't think he's interested, Iris, and I can't for the life of me figure out why you had me call him."

"Because, dear, he asked me to," she insisted. Tracey was being particularly tiresome about all this. Why couldn't she just do as Iris wished? Well, there was more than one way to skin a cat, she thought to herself. Time for phase two of her plan.

"Maybe he was busy," Tracey suggested, "but he seemed as if he was just being polite to me, that's all."

"I'm sure he was," Iris replied. "He was probably so pleased to hear your voice he didn't know what to say. That's why we have to try again."

"Shouldn't we just leave this alone?" Tracey suggested. "I mean, he does sound happy. Let's just let it go."

"No, no," she reprimanded. "Daddy's being coy, that's all. I know he's not happy at all. He tells me so every time I see him. Actually, he's wretched. He needs someone like you." She paused and then launched into phase two. "Why don't you come to Bay City for an extended visit as my guest? I'd love to have you."

"And leave Washington and all my friends at Christmastime?"

"Now, Tracey," Iris began in her most convincing tone. "You've told me yourself that you're getting tired of Washington. All those same, dreary faces, you said. Why not come here for a while? I have a wonderful new house with a guest wing and you'd be the first to stay in it. We'll have such fun at all the festivities." *And I'll make such lovely trouble,* Iris completed the sentence to herself.

"But didn't you say that Bay City was very quiet? What would we do?"

"Oh, there's scads of things to do —especially during the holiday season. But, really, I'm getting lonesome for my old friends. And don't you want to meet my new husband?"

Tracey had to laugh. She did wonder about this new husband. He had to be a very brave man to have married her. "The thought has crossed my mind. Is he very good looking, Iris?"

"Would I marry someone who wasn't?" she chided her. "Of course he's fantastically good looking. And charming. And wonderful. And—" She would have gone on but Tracey interrupted her.

"All right. You've piqued my curiosity. I'll come."

"Oh, good!" Iris exclaimed excitedly. "When should I expect you?"

"Well, there are some things I have to tie up here. And then I have to pack and close the apartment. How about in a week's time?"

"A week!" Iris groaned. "I was thinking more along the lines of tomorrow."

"Tomorrow!" Now it was Tracey's turn to groan. "I could never get everything done by tomorrow."

"Then the day after."

"Iris, be reasonable."

"Never," Iris retorted. "I am never reasonable. You have to come the day after tomorrow."

"I'll try," she said, sighing. "But all that packing . . ."

"I know dear, it's bothersome. But whatever you forget we'll just buy here. Besides," she continued, "that will just give us another excuse to go on a glorious shopping spree. Remember when we used to do that?"

"I remember, Iris," she said, grinning. If there was one thing Iris knew how to do, it was shop. She spent money faster and better than anyone she knew, probably better than anyone else on the face of the earth. "But I'm not as young as I used to be. We'll have to take breaks."

Iris laughed. It was a hearty laugh and she was surprised at how good it made her feel to respond honestly about something. "There's a lovely little tearoom downtown that's perfect for taking breaks between splurges. They have the most delicious éclairs."

"All right, you've sold me," Tracey admitted. After all, she rationalized, Iris could be a great deal of fun when she was in one of her good moods.

"The day after tomorrow, then?"

"I'll call you with my flight number when I have it," Tracey promised.

"Wonderful. I can hardly wait."

"Me too." Tracey said good-bye and then hung up.

Iris rose from her chair and clasped her hands together in triumph.

"I *can* hardly wait," she repeated to herself, and then practically dove into the clothing laid out on her bed. There were so many things to be done before Tracey arrived. Suddenly, she relished all the little odds and ends she'd have to take care of for her friend's arrival.

They were going to have fun. So much fun. And the most fun of all was going to be watching Rachel's face when she finally met Tracey DeWitt.

Chapter Eight
No Other Way Out

Marianne Randolph stepped off the elevator, and with uneven, nervous steps, approached the receptionist of her father's law firm. Behind the receptionist's desk, a huge plate-glass window offered a view overlooking the bay. Clouds skittered across a perfectly blue sky, playing hide-and-seek with the sun, which was unusually bright for mid-December.

But the sight, which usually made her happy to be alive and proud to be the daughter of a partner in one of Bay City's most prestigious law firms, only made her more nervous and unhappy. She was there to tell her father the truth. But how could she tell him she was pregnant, unmarried, and abandoned by a man he had never liked, when he'd spent most of his life working hard so she could have everything she had ever wanted or needed? How could she disappoint him, when he'd never let her down once in her life? He was a perfect father, and always had been.

All these thoughts raced through her head as she approached the receptionist.

"Hi, Marianne," the perky young woman greeted her. "If you're here to see your dad you're going to have to wait a bit. He's out on business."

Marianne almost turned on her heel and left again, wanting to believe that this was an omen that she shouldn't tell him her secret, that he would be better off not knowing, but she was stopped by a friendly voice.

"Marianne Randolph!" A lovely, petite brunette with a friendly smile approached her from behind.

Marianne turned. "Hello, Barbara," she greeted in a small voice.

Barbara Weaver was a young associate in her father's firm who worked with him mostly on Frame Enterprise business. Barbara had been to the Randolphs' home several times and was acquainted with Marianne, but just barely. She didn't have to know Marianne very well, however, to sense she wasn't happy. "Your dad's supposed to be back at the office any minute now," she offered helpfully. "I know because I have a meeting with him in half an hour."

"It sounds as if he's busy," Marianne observed, beginning to inch away from her. "Maybe I'll come back." Why had she ever thought that coming to his office and telling him there was the way to handle this problem? She should have known that he'd be too busy to see her.

"No, don't do that." Barbara placed a delaying hand on her arm. "Come to my office. We can chat and you can wait for him there."

"Well . . ." Marianne said, continuing to hedge away. "When he gets back he'll want to see you. Not me."

Barbara shook her head. "You're saying he won't want to see his favorite daughter?" she asked, and then immediately regretted what she'd said, seeing Marianne's suddenly stricken face. What could possibly be wrong? She decided to take matters into her own hands. "Come on." She grabbed Marianne's arm and pulled her down the hall. "We'll talk."

Reluctantly, Marianne let herself be dragged to Barbara's office. What could they possibly have to talk about? she wondered. They hardly knew each other.

When she reached her office, Barbara steered Marianne to a chair across from her desk, then sat in the other chair opposite it. "You must be getting ready for finals, aren't you?" she asked politely.

Marianne gave her a blank look.

"Didn't you register at Bay State this semester?" Barbara asked.

She shook her head. "Michael did."

"But I thought your father said you both were going to register," Barbara replied, puzzled.

Marianne sighed. This was just another of the things she had done, or rather not done in this case, to disappoint her father. "I put it off a semester."

"Not ready?"

"I had other things on my mind." *Mainly Chris Peterson,* she completed the sentence to herself. What a mistake that had been.

"Well, good for you," Barbara congratulated her.

Startled, Marianne shot her a quizzical look.

"I mean, good for you that you knew you weren't ready, yet. A lot of people would have gone anyhow and not done as well as they could have if they'd waited until they were sure. Good for you that you knew your own mind."

Looking at Barbara to see if she was being honest, Marianne observed that her face was kind and her reactions were sincere. Her defensiveness toward her began to disappear. "But Dad wasn't happy about it," she admitted. "He thought it was foolish."

Barbara laughed ruefully. "Parents always think they know best, don't they? My parents thought I should have been a teacher. That was a useful profession to them. They think all lawyers are sharks preying on the innocent." She laughed again. "Well, here I am—a shark. They don't think it's so bad now that they can send their friends to me when they have legal problems and I'll help them for free. So I turned out all right, after all."

Marianne smiled, barely.

Observing Marianne's pinched and unhappy face, Barbara turned serious. Joking her out of her bad mood wasn't going to work, she could see that. "Marianne, I don't like to pry, but is something wrong?"

She shook her head no, then nodded, then shook her head again.

"It can't be that you're just feeling badly about not going to school when your father wanted you to," Barbara prodded gently. "Or is that just a part of it?"

Surprised at Barbara's perceptiveness, Marianne broke down. "I'm such a disappointment to him," she whispered, ashamed to admit it.

"But you're not!" Barbara protested. "I don't know how many times John has praised you to me. He thinks you're the smartest, prettiest, nicest young lady around. Granted, he's prejudiced," she continued, "but he truly loves you. You couldn't disappoint him."

"But I have," Marianne repudiated her

claims quietly. "That's why I'm here. To tell him what I've done."

"What could you have done that could be that bad?" Barbara asked with a joking lilt to her voice. She had been quite worried about Marianne when she first saw her, but now she thought that perhaps Marianne and her father had probably just had a little argument about something, which she had blown all out of proportion. Barbara remembered how oversensitive she had been at that age.

She really wasn't prepared for what Marianne told her.

"Barbara, I'm pregnant. My boyfriend has left town and he wants nothing to do with me or the baby. I think I'm going to have an abortion." Marianne kept her voice even to keep her feelings from breaking through.

"Oh, Marianne . . ." Barbara reacted by reaching out to her and touching her hand sympathetically.

"I've told Mom and my brother, but they insist I have to tell Dad, too." She paused and then went on. "But I'm so scared, Barbara. I'm so afraid he'll be disappointed in me." Her voice began to crack with emotion. "I couldn't stand that."

Barbara nodded her head. "But you're here, Marianne. You're going to tell him and that takes courage," she offered.

"I don't think he'll see it that way," replied Marianne, grateful for the encouragement but not convinced by it. "My father always expected me to be a virgin until I married."

"And I suppose you did, too, didn't you?"

"Yes, I did," Marianne replied. "But then I met Chris."

"And everything you thought went up into thin air."

Marianne turned a pair of very surprised eyes to her. "Yes, that's exactly right. How did you know?"

Barbara shrugged good-naturedly. "I've fallen in love too, Marianne. You never know what will happen when you fall in love. You can do some pretty foolish things."

"But you didn't get pregnant, did you?" Marianne asked sadly.

"I could have," Barbara responded frankly, "but I didn't. I was lucky I suppose."

"I guess I wasn't very lucky, was I?" Marianne said, then began to cry. At this point, she didn't know if there would ever be a day when she wouldn't cry.

"No, you weren't," Barbara agreed honestly. "But sometimes we're lucky and sometimes we're not. It can't be helped. That's how life is." She went over to Marianne and wrapped a protective arm around her. "But it will turn out all right. You have to believe that."

"I wish I could." Marianne wiped the tears from her face. It wouldn't do to let her father see her crying before she even told him what was wrong.

"Are you sure about the abortion?" Barbara asked gently. "That's a big decision."

"I don't see any other way, but I know my father won't want me to do it."

Barbara nodded in agreement. She didn't know John very well, but she did know that he had very strong ideas about those kinds of things. Most fathers did.

"I don't think I'm going to tell him about that," Marianne decided. After seeing Barbara nod so surely, she knew her suspicion had been correct.

"But you'll have to," Barbara insisted. "He'll want to know."

"I'll tell him afterward."

"But that's a little too late, isn't it?"

"What choice do I have?" Marianne cried.

"Marianne, you have to be honest with your father. He expects that from you."

"He expected other things, too, didn't he?" Marianne cried in agitation. "And I've let him down. What difference does it make at this point? Don't you understand that, Barbara?" Looking at the clock, she rose to leave. Her father was already almost half an hour late.

Not wanting Marianne to leave on such a pessimistic note, Barbara pushed her back down onto the chair. "I do understand," she protested. "But I can't tell you that I approve of your doing something that is going to estrange you from your father. He'll be devastated if you do this thing and don't tell him ahead of time."

"How can I tell him," Marianne asked, "when he isn't even here?" She was beginning to feel slightly hysterical. To come here and tell him was hard enough, but to have to wait to no avail was unbearably difficult.

"He'll be here," Barbara assured her. "He's just tied up."

"I can't wait any longer." Marianne stood up again. "Please don't tell him what I've told you. Don't even tell him that I've been here." She ran out of the office.

"Marianne!" Barbara called after her, but it did no good. She was already out of hearing distance.

Mere moments later, when John Randolph entered Barbara's office and began their meeting, he wondered why she was being especially kind to him. Several times during their conference he thought of asking her why, but then decided it was just her way. She was an extraordinarily sympathetic young woman, besides being an excellent lawyer, and she was lovely to look at, too.

Funny, he hadn't really noticed that before.

Marianne pulled her car over to the curb. She had barely gotten out of the parking lot next to her father's building when she realized she could hardly see to drive. The tears welling in her eyes made everything look as bleary as she felt.

It had been so difficult to bring herself to her father's office, and then for him not to show up . . . She knew she shouldn't feel as if he had abandoned her since he had had no way of knowing she had been there waiting for him, but she did harbor resentment, irrational as it was. Why hadn't he been there when she needed him?

Now she was so shaken she didn't think she'd ever be able to get up the courage to retry her effort—especially since she'd sensed that Barbara Weaver also believed her father would never permit her to have an abortion. Barbara hardly even knew her father, and she could still be sure about that!

She leaned back in the car seat, and then slumped sideways, pressing her hot cheek against the cool glass of the window. Her breath made a light, foggy film on the glass as she watched people scurrying up and down Bay City's Main Street, carrying brightly wrapped packages as they went about their Christmas shopping.

Christmas! Marianne sighed. It had always been the happiest time of the year for her. It meant presents piled up under the tree, and family dinners with aunts and uncles and cousins and grandparents in attendance, and Christmas caroling to all the neighbors' houses, and hot cider and popcorn as they decorated the big tree in the living room, trying to make it even grander and more beautiful than it had been the year before. Christmas was when everybody forgot all their petty annoyances and trifling problems and joined the joyful spirit around them.

But now Marianne knew that this Christmas wasn't going to be like any of the others, at least, not for her.

She restarted the car and aimed it back onto the street, heading for her brother's apartment. She had made up her mind about what she was going to do. Now all she needed was Michael and Glenda to help her see it through.

Michael frowned when his sister finished her story. "I don't like this, sis. I don't like it at all."

She wrung her hands. "If I can't count on you, Michael, who can I count on?"

Glenda placed a hand on his arm. "Look, why don't you let me help?" she suggested.

He sighed. "Whether or not it's you or

me who helps, it still boils down to the same thing, Glenda. We're lying to my parents." He was beginning to feel like a broken record with his sister. Repeatedly he had cajoled her to be honest and to tell the truth, when in fact, he hadn't been doing it himself.

He supposed that if he really meant what he said he would have told his father days ago what was happening to his sister. But as twins, the bond between his sister and himself was so strong that he supposed he would always be more loyal to her than to probably anyone else he would ever know. If she asked him to lie for her, he would. He wouldn't be happy about it, he would hate himself for doing it, but he would do it all the same.

"They don't give Marianne much choice, do they, Michael?" Glenda asked softly.

"What do you mean?" he replied defensively.

"She has decided that she doesn't want to have this baby. But your mother insists that she does. And you all seem pretty positive that your father will feel the same way. Should Marianne be forced to have a baby that she doesn't want just because her parents want to decide her life for her?"

"That's beside the point, Glenda. She's keeping something from them. She's betraying their trust."

"And what about Marianne's trust? Doesn't she have the right to expect her parents' support when she makes a decision? Shouldn't they have enough trust in her to believe she's capable of making the right decision? Why do they think they know better?"

Michael looked at his sister. "Are you sure that this is what you want to do?" he asked in a resigned voice.

Numbly, Marianne nodded her head. She felt so tired, so weary of reviewing over and over in her head the same questions with the same answers. It was like a jigsaw puzzle that would always be lacking one of its pieces to make the picture whole. Whichever way she figured it, the picture would always have a wide, aching gap in it. Nothing she could do would ever make it right.

Michael looked at Glenda. "Call the clinic," he said. "You'd better set up an appointment."

When she went into the other room to make the call, Michael and Marianne stayed where they were, neither of them saying a word to each other until she returned.

"It's set," she said in an even voice. "It's for December twenty-sixth."

"The day after Christmas," Marianne murmured, almost to herself.

"They want you to check in with them a

couple days ahead of time for some routine tests," Glenda informed her.

"You mean I'll have to be in New York for Christmas?" Marianne asked, obviously unhappy.

Glenda sighed. "I'm afraid so. But you can stay with me if you like at my parents' home. They won't mind. In fact, they'd love to meet Michael's sister."

"How are you going to explain this to Mom and Dad?" he inquired. "You know they'll figure out that something's wrong if you tell them you won't be home for Christmas."

"I'm not going to tell them," she replied.

He threw his head back and, astounded, cried, "Marianne!"

"Michael," Glenda said, raising her voice to him, "what else can she do? They'll stop her if she tells them."

"I just can't believe this. It keeps going from bad to worse."

Guiltily, Marianne took a step toward her brother. "I know you're not happy with me, Michael, but I can't help that. I have to do what I feel is right. Please don't be angry." Gently, she placed a hand on his sleeve and tugged.

When Michael looked down at his sister's face and saw the hurt and pain it contained, he immediately regretted his angry words. "Oh, sis," he said, wrapping his arms around her and giving her a tender hug, "I'm not mad."

"I'm so sorry about all this," she said and began to cry.

"No, I'm sorry," he said as he stroked her hair. "I'm sorry I've been giving you such a hard time." He held her until her body stopped shivering with sobs, then let her go.

"I guess I better go home and start packing," she said. "I'll have to do it in bits and pieces so Mom doesn't notice."

"We're going to have to leave tomorrow, Marianne, late in the afternoon so you can be at the clinic first thing the next morning for those tests," Glenda advised. "I'll make the plane reservations."

Marianne nodded and turned to leave. "Will I see you tomorrow?" she asked her brother as he accompanied her to the door.

He shook his head. "I've got finals all day long."

"Oh." Marianne stood on the threshold of his front door. "Well, then," she began, throwing her arms around him, "merry Christmas, Michael."

"Merry Christmas, Marianne."

Chapter Nine
The Truth Comes Out

Bay City basked in the glow of an unseasonably mild day for mid-December as Rachel parked the car in Iris's driveway. She was about to enter the path to the front door when she heard voices coming from the patio. She cut around to the side of the house instead of ringing at the front. It would make her visit more casual and friendly, she thought, to just present herself rather than wait for Iris's maid to answer the door and announce her.

Several days had passed since she'd resolved to speak to Iris. Jamie had come down with a cold due to the erratic weather they'd been having and she'd been so concerned with him that she hadn't been able to get away. And, to be truthful, as much as she wanted to extend her friendship to Iris she was apprehensive about the meeting. She knew it wouldn't be easy to convince her of her sincerity.

She was just about to step up to the patio when she heard another voice answer Iris's, a voice she had never heard before. Not wanting to interrupt, she began to head around to the front again so she could be announced properly, but was stopped in her tracks by Iris's next declaration.

"Tracey," she was stating, "I had to marry him for his own good."

Rachel stood rooted to the spot. Who else could it be on Iris's patio but Tracey DeWitt. What was she doing in Bay City?

"What do you mean?" she heard Tracey ask.

"It was that horrid girl, Clarice," Iris drawled. "She isn't our kind at all. Not the kind of girl that Robert should be involved with. I suppose he took up with her in a moment of weakness. And then the silly goose got herself pregnant. So you see, I had to put a stop to it."

Rachel leaned against the wall for support. So that's how it was! She could hardly believe her ears. She had always known that Iris was capable of almost anything when she put her mind to it. But this . . . Poor Clarice! Poor Robert!

"Do you think that was wise, Iris?" Tracey inquired. "Sometimes it's best to leave these things alone."

"And let that dreary girl ruin Robert's life? No, no." Rachel imagined that Iris was waving her hand to dismiss utterly the idea of leaving something that didn't agree with her alone. "I offered the creature all the money she could possibly want to leave Bay City and start over somewhere new. She wouldn't take it. Her idea of pride, I suppose."

"But what if Robert finds out about the baby?" Tracey asked.

Iris laughed abruptly. "He'll never find out. I certainly won't tell him and neither will Clarice. I made sure of that."

"How?"

Rachel stood on her toes and leaned closer to the edge of the wall to make sure she heard Iris's answer. What *had* she done?

"I really can't say," Iris murmured evasively. "Let's just say that she will never tell him. And you can't tell him either," she instructed Tracey. "We're very happy now. He has everything he needs. Why would he want to know about a child he had with a woman he doesn't even care about anymore?"

So that was it! Finally, Rachel understood Clarice's stubbornness in not telling Robert that he was Cory's father. She didn't doubt that what Iris wasn't saying was that she'd threatened Clarice in some way, made her so afraid of what she would do if she told Robert, that she was determined to carry her secret to the grave rather than risk Iris's wrath. What an evil woman Iris was!

"But let's not talk about that anymore. It's all over and done with, after all. Let's talk about you. And Daddy." Iris's voice had taken on a distinctly wheedling tone.

It wasn't bad enough, Rachel thought, that Iris wanted to ruin Clarice and Robert's lives, now she was determined to ruin hers and Mac's.

It was all perfectly clear now. First Iris had tried to stir up something in Washington, and when that hadn't worked, she'd brought Tracey to Bay City. And to think that Rachel had come by just to patch things up between herself and Iris! It was a good thing she'd overheard this little conversation. Now she knew that the only way to treat Iris was as an enemy. There seemed to be no limit to her treachery or her tricks.

But she was surprised by Tracey's reply to Iris's suggestion.

"Oh, Iris, not today. I've barely settled in yet. In fact, I'm still not unpacked. I think I'll do that now." Tracey excused herself.

"You do that, dear," Iris called to her as she left the patio. "And then we'll have lunch downtown."

Perhaps Tracey wasn't going to be the willing accomplice Iris had hoped for, Rachel thought. Judging from her voice she sounded like a nice woman. And Rachel doubted that Mac had ever once cared for someone who wasn't. The thought that Iris might be fooling herself put a little spring in her step as she reapproached the patio from her hiding spot near the side wall.

"Hello, Iris," she called to her back as she stepped up to the patio.

Iris turned with a start. "My goodness, you startled me. There's a front door, you know," she grumbled.

"I heard you out back, so I just thought I'd skip the front door."

Rachel noticed Iris's eyes narrowing, and she knew she was wondering just what it was she'd heard. And then Iris shrugged, as if she couldn't care less.

"You're looking well," she complimented Rachel, then pulled it back by adding, "considering."

"Well, you know what they say, pregnancy's a condition, not a sickness." Now that she knew what Iris was up to she felt blissfully in control of things. She could let Iris's insults slide off her back like a duck shaking off water. She was prepared.

"Hmmm," Iris murmured as she wiped a crumb off her sweater. It was a tweedy, hand-knit designer creation, and it must have cost a small fortune. "I found pregnancy dreary. The clothes were so ordinary." She sniffed as she gave her father's wife a going over.

"These are just my regular ordinary clothes," Rachel tossed back. "I'm not into maternity yet." She gave Iris a big smile.

For the life of her, Iris couldn't figure out why Rachel was being so cheerful. Usually, one of her insults was enough to ruin her day. The woman was being maddeningly resilient, but she couldn't let that stop her from trying to get under her skin.

"Maybe you're just one of those women who are meant to be pregnant, dear. The kind who have nothing else of value in their lives so they have one after the other. Like an assembly line," Iris chirped brightly.

This, Rachel decided, was starting to get annoying. She decided it was time to take the offensive. "I'm enjoying this pregnancy, Iris. In fact, I'm enjoying it so much I can't see why anyone wouldn't want to be pregnant. Like you, for instance." That should get the ball rolling. She had decided that it was time to call Iris on her treatment of Clarice. Perhaps she'd think twice about pulling any more tricks.

"Me?" She was so startled by the suggestion she nearly dropped the cup she had balanced in her fingers.

"Why not?" Rachel countered. "You and Robert might like to have a child."

"I assure you, that's the last thing on my

mind." She placed her cup firmly on the tray.

"And Robert?" Rachel asked cagily.

"He has Dennis now. That's enough." She was beginning to look distinctly uneasy.

"Oh?" Rachel raised her eyebrows. "I thought every man likes to have a child of his own."

"Not Robert," Iris said with finality. "He doesn't want a child."

"Is that why you married him, then?"

Iris turned a quizzical face to her. What *was* she getting at?

"Did you marry him to keep him from having a child? His child with Clarice?" Rachel accused.

"How do you—" Iris nearly blurted out the truth but stopped herself and changed her tune. "I don't know what you mean." She clutched her cardigan about her as if she were about to leave.

"I mean that you knew Clarice was pregnant and you snatched Robert away from her," Rachel declared with relish.

Suddenly Iris realized how she had discovered the truth. "Why, you snoop!" she exclaimed. "You've been eavesdropping. How common!"

"Let's just say I overheard a conversation," Rachel corrected her. "You may have scared Clarice with your threats, but you can't scare me. I've half a mind to stop by Robert's office right now and tell him what you've been up to."

"I wouldn't do that, Rachel dear." She was very calm now.

"Why not? He should know the truth."

"If you overheard my conversation about Robert, then you're also aware of with whom I was having that conversation, aren't you?"

"Yes, Iris, I know you've brought Tracey DeWitt up here to stir up some trouble between Mac and me. But it won't work."

"Oh, you'd be surprised," Iris hinted maliciously.

"No, Iris, you'll be surprised. Because I'm going to tell Mac exactly what you're up to."

"He won't believe you," she answered with conviction. "He rarely does, you know."

Rachel wavered. She was partly right. Mac always found it difficult to believe the treachery his daughter was capable of. "I'll make him," she said with false bravado.

"You won't succeed. Besides, he would never believe that Tracey would come to Bay City just to cause difficulties. He loved her very much. He has a very high opinion of her character."

"You're using her, Iris. She's probably a very nice woman and you're using her to make unhappiness. Is that how you treat your friends?"

Iris ignored her accusation. "She's visiting Bay City because she's bored in Washington," she said, half believing her own lie. "Naturally she won't be able to avoid Mac. He is my father after all. Then—" she paused for dramatic effect "—we'll just have to see what happens."

"Nothing will happen."

"As I said," Iris said, rising to leave, "we'll see. Tracey is a beautiful woman. Men tend to take notice."

Rachel also rose and began to follow her into the house. "I'm warning you, Iris . . ."

Iris turned on her in fury. "And I'm warning *you*, Rachel. If you ever breathe a word of this business to Robert or anyone, I'll ruin you. I've never liked you. You'll never be good enough for my father, and I'll never stop until I've broken up your marriage."

Rachel was shocked at the venom in Iris's attack. It practically took her breath away. She saw Iris's face, distorted with anger and hatred, and she realized she meant what she said. But she was damned if she'd let her know that she was afraid.

"As you said, Iris, we'll see." She threw the words in her face, then turned her back and left.

Iris watched as Rachel strode purposefully away from the patio. It was false courage, she knew. No woman could be that sure of her man. And what did Rachel have to fight with? She was just a gold digger who had gotten lucky and struck it rich.

Her marriage to Mac wouldn't last long. Because, Iris vowed, she'd do her best to make sure it didn't.

"Rachel, you've been quiet as a mouse all evening. Is something wrong?" Mac asked.

She put down the brush she'd been stroking her hair with and watched her husband in the mirror of the vanity. It had always been difficult to keep her feelings from him. He was so sensitive to her moods.

"Won't you tell me? he implored. "I'm all yours."

"Are you, Mac?" she asked.

He turned her around on the vanity seat, then knelt next to her. "Why on earth would you ask that? You know the answer."

She looked into his eyes. They were so kind, so full of love. "Yes, I guess I do," she conceded.

"You guess?" he chided. "I love you. I will always love you. And now I love you even more," he murmured softly and touched her face with his hand. "This baby means the world to me."

"And to me," she agreed, taking his hand and holding it in hers.

"Then what's the problem?" he beseeched.

"I stopped by Iris's today," she began. She wouldn't tell him everything that had happened between herself and Iris, but she did feel she should warn him about Bay City's newest arrival.

"Ah, that's right. Didn't your reconciliation attempt work?"

"You know Iris," she offered, shaking her head.

Rising, he paced over to the bedroom window and leaned against the sill. "Give her time. She'll come around."

Rachel shrugged. "But that's not why I've been so quiet this evening."

He raised an eyebrow.

"Tracey DeWitt is staying at Iris's. She's come up from Washington."

"Well, they were very good friends once. They're probably just catching up with each other."

Rachel took a deep breath to launch into the real reason why Iris had brought Tracey to Bay City, but then changed her mind. Mac wouldn't want to believe that Iris could hate her so much that she'd be willing to ruin her father's life just to make Rachel's miserable. After all, what parent would want to know their child capable of that kind of treachery? Not wanting to hurt him in any way, even though it would mean subduing Iris, she decided to keep silent.

Instead she said, "I suppose that's true," and left it at that. She rose and headed over to the bed, where she turned down the spread.

Mac came up behind her and wrapped

her in his arms. "Tracey DeWitt holds no charms for me," he whispered in her ear, his breath ruffling her hair.

She turned so she was facing him. "There aren't any embers smoldering away in there?" She patted the place over his heart.

He grabbed her hand and put it up to his lips. "They burned out a long time ago. And if they hadn't, the fire you started would have engulfed them." He clasped her to him tightly.

"Then there's nothing to worry about?" she whispered, needing his reassurance.

"Not a thing," he replied as he began to nibble at her neck.

Rachel let herself succumb to the delicious sensation of his lips on her skin, but a small part of her resisted. Deep inside there was a part of her that was afraid, so afraid that what Mac wanted and wished for, what she wanted and wished for, meant little in the face of Iris's determination to tear them apart. She was afraid that Iris would succeed, that not even a love as strong as the one she and Mac shared could survive a hatred as strong as Iris's.

Hours later, when the night was still and quiet, Mac slept, but Rachel was still wide awake.

It wasn't herself and Mac she was thinking about anymore. Their lovemaking had laid to rest her fears, at least for the moment. It was Clarice and Robert she now considered.

Now that she knew the truth about Iris's part in Clarice's troubles she wondered if that knowledge didn't bring its own set of responsibilities.

She was debating telling Clarice that she knew of Iris's threats, and then pleading with her to ignore them and tell Robert what he so desperately wanted to know. After all, what else could Iris do to Clarice? She'd already taken the father of her child away from her and estranged him from his son. What could be worse?

Rachel pondered the problem for a minute. There really was no way to know what Iris could or would do. Her ability to stir up trouble was unfathomable. She could fix things so that Clarice would lose her job or her apartment, or perhaps even lose her son. But at least, she countered this argument, Robert would know and Iris wouldn't get away with her despicable scheme. In fact, Robert's love for Clarice might even be renewed once he knew.

But then, what kind of a future could Clarice and Robert ever have with Iris in the wings? She'd never divorce Robert; she'd never let him be free to be with his son and the mother of his child. It occurred to Rachel that the consequences of Robert's discovering the truth about Cory

—as well as the truth about Iris—could make for an even more miserable existence than he already had not knowing. And it probably wouldn't make life any easier for Clarice.

Rachel turned restlessly. Wasn't there anything she could do? It disturbed her to think that Cory, a vulnerable child, would eventually be the one who suffered the most. He would never know his father.

How could Iris do something like this? She was a mother. She ought to have had some sympathy for the child she was using as a pawn in her game to win Robert.

It was with a twinge of recognition that Rachel twisted and then sat straight up in bed. What was that old saying? People in glass houses shouldn't throw stones.

She rose and went over to the window and sat on the seat beneath it. Gazing out on the meadow leading down to the lake as it lay dappled in moonlight, she mulled over the thought that she actually had no right to castigate Iris for her part in Clarice and Robert's troubles. Hadn't she once done the same kind of meddling herself?

She had used her own son, Jamie, to break up Steve Frame's marriage to Alice Matthews. She had told Alice, so happy on the day of her engagement, that the baby she was carrying wasn't her own husband's but the child of a man she had slept with only once. Only once because she had caught Steve in a weak and vulnerable moment one night.

She had known that Steve truly loved Alice, but she hadn't cared. Rachel had wanted him more than anything she'd ever wanted before in her life, and she wasn't going to let true love or someone else's happiness stand in her way of getting him.

So who was she to scourge Iris for having no conscience in her efforts to keep her husband? Rachel had once caused just as much unhappiness.

Wearily, she dragged herself back to bed. It was no use trying to figure out a solution to this problem with Robert and Clarice. The only person who could do anything was Clarice, and she'd made her decision. Rachel would just have to live with that, despite what she knew.

But what if . . . what if . . . Her mind kept going over the options as she tried to relax her body and welcome sleep. Perhaps the best decision to make would be to sleep and reconsider it all in the morning.

With a heavy sigh, she turned and snuggled up against Mac. He rustled in his sleep, automatically throwing an arm over her body and pulling her closer.

When that happened, she knew she had made the right decision. Sleep, with all its oblivion, came shortly after.

Chapter Ten
A Breach of Trust

The warm spell had departed Bay City just as suddenly as it had arrived, and as Michael approached his parents' house from the sidewalk, snow was just beginning to fall. It swirled around him, lightly billowing and rising and dropping in the air until it settled on the ground, covering the brown, stubbly grass and a few mounds of leaves still left over from autumn. It was the first serious snowfall of the season. The weather forecasters were predicting a white Christmas.

In the windows of the Randolph house Pat had already lit the white candles she placed there every year. Michael could see them glowing through the twilight mist of snow. When he opened the front door he

155

knew there would be smells of evergreen and cinnamon and cider warming on the stove, scenting the whole house with what, to him, would always be the smell of Christmas.

It was the night before Christmas Eve and Michael was coming home to tell his parents that his sister wouldn't be spending the holiday with them. Earlier that afternoon she and Glenda had boarded the plane to New York, escaping just before the snow began. Michael had been left behind to break the news.

He tried not to imagine ahead of time what his parents' reaction was going to be. If he did, he knew he'd never be able to enter the house. Squaring his shoulders, he turned the knob of the front door and pressed forward with a smile of fake Christmas cheer on his face.

His mother was draping a bit of garland on the lowest bough of the tree.

"Michael!" she exclaimed, pleased and surprised to see her son earlier than she'd expected. "Where's Glenda? Is she coming later?"

Now it began. He returned his mother's kiss and then informed her that Glenda wouldn't be coming at all since she'd already left for her family's home in New York.

"Oh, that's too bad," she sympathized, thinking that Michael looked so down in the dumps because he wouldn't be spending Christmas with his girlfriend. "But she probably only gets to see her parents once during the school year, doesn't she?"

He nodded. Oh, how he was dreading this conversation.

"They're not lucky like we are," Pat continued. "We get to see you and Marianne all year round." She attached the end of the garland to a branch at the back of the tree, then stood back to judge its effect. She must have liked it because she smiled.

Michael thought his mother looked happier than she had in days and he told her so.

Pat smiled. "I'm going to be a grandmother, Michael. I've known that for a while, but I just realized today what that meant."

A chill went down Michael's back. What in the world was going on?

"All this time I've been so worried and upset about Chris Peterson's leaving town and Marianne's being pregnant without a husband that I hadn't even considered the fun there's going to be having a new addition to this family. The very first grandchild for John and me." She plucked an ornament off the tree, then put it back just a millimeter to the right of where it had been. "It's not the way I imagined I'd be welcoming my first grandchild, but that's not the child's fault is it? And we have to think of the child first, don't we?"

Michael listened in horror. "Mom, what are you talking about?" he asked, finally finding his voice.

She turned to him and motioned with her finger to the closet. "This morning I was looking for some of the Christmas decorations," she said as she walked over to the closet door and waved Michael along with her, "and I found this." She pulled open the door, rummaged on the back shelf, and presented a package wrapped in paper with little pink and blue storks all over it.

Michael's jaw dropped.

His mother laughed melodiously. "I know it's not nice to pry but I couldn't resist when I saw the paper." Carefully, she hid it back on the shelf and closed the door. "It's a sweater set for Marianne's baby. She must have bought it when she decided she wasn't going to go through with the abortion. Michael, she's going to keep the baby."

He said nothing. He wasn't ready yet to burst the lovely little bubble of happiness upon which his mother was so precariously perching. It would be crushing when he finally told her the truth.

"Aren't you excited?" Pat asked him. "You'll be an uncle!"

He stared at her, his face holding an expression of love and horror. He would have begun to tell her the truth, but just at that moment his father opened the front door.

"Merry Christmas!" he bellowed to Michael as he deposited a pile of gaily wrapped presents on the foyer table. He approached Pat and gave her a quick, affectionate peck on the cheek. "You, too!" he said, and winked.

When John had returned from work before going out again to Christmas shop, he had noticed that his wife's mood had gone through a remarkable change. That morning when he'd left she'd been as down as he'd ever seen her, although still protesting that nothing was wrong. But this afternoon, she'd been practically glowing with happiness. All she'd said was that she'd told him her mood would pass and it had.

Pat put her hands up to her husband's cheeks. "Frosty," she noted. "How about some hot chocolate?" She turned to Michael. "You, too?"

Both men nodded.

"I'll be back in a jiffy," she said, walking toward the kitchen.

"Where's that pretty girlfriend of yours, Michael?" John asked as he sat down in his easy chair and motioned for Michael to sit opposite him on the couch. "I thought she was going to help with the tree tonight, too."

"She's gone to stay with her parents."

"And where's your sister?" his father asked next. "Your mother thought she might be out shopping, but I didn't see her at any of the stores. I thought she was probably with you cooking up some kind of Christmas surprise. Or have you two gotten too old for that?" John laughed. "I remember the year you decided you were going to be Santa Claus and climb down the chimney, and we had to call the fire department to get you off the roof when you realized you were never going to fit. I'll never forget the look on Marianne's face when she had to tell us what you'd done."

Was his father a mind reader, Michael wondered? He just smiled.

"So, she's not with you," John observed. "I wonder where she is?"

Michael took a deep breath. "She's on the plane with Glenda," he announced.

"On the plane with Glenda?" John repeated, incredulously. "Why is she doing that? If this is her idea of a Christmas surprise, it's not very funny."

"What's not funny?" Pat asked, as she entered the living room with mugs of steaming hot chocolate on a silver tray.

"Michael says Marianne is on a plane to New York," John told her as she approached the coffee table to put the tray down.

"What!" She would have dropped the tray on the floor if the coffee table hadn't been just underneath it. She fell onto the couch on the other side of Michael and put a hand up to her head as if she felt faint.

Michael saw her look over to the closet, then at him, then back at the closet again. Her face was drained of all its color. He looked away.

"She's staying with Glenda's parents for the holidays," he said to the space above the fireplace's mantelpiece. He couldn't meet either of his parents' eyes.

"But we always have Christmas together," John protested, trying to make some sense of the news. "And I don't understand why she'd just leave and not bother to tell us what she intended to do."

"I can," Pat whispered, so softly that only Michael, who was sitting the closest to her, could hear.

He turned and faced her, his heart pounding in his chest as hard as he'd ever felt it. Her eyes, when she aimed them at him, were hard with accusation.

In only a few seconds, Pat found what she sought in her son's face. His expression confirmed her fear, and her expression, in return, confirmed that she knew what Michael wasn't telling her. Marianne had gone to New York to have an abortion.

Now, Michael wondered as his mother leaned back on the couch with a numbed expression on her face, will she tell Dad?

"I just don't understand her at all," his

father continued. He also didn't understand his son's nervousness or his wife's state of shock. Although he didn't like Marianne's absence, he felt it was something Michael shouldn't feel responsible for and Pat shouldn't take so seriously.

Michael cleared his throat. "I think she just wanted a break, that's all, Dad. Bay City can get kind of dull sometimes. It's always the same old thing," he rambled on as if he thought he might start making some sense if he just kept at it.

"The same old thing is what we call Christmas tradition in this family, Michael," his father reminded him. "I can see why she might want to get away, but not at Christmastime."

"Well, that's the only time Glenda goes back to New York City, so it was either go now, or not go at all," he explained, amazed at what a good liar he could be on such short notice.

"She probably didn't want to tell us," his mother finally said, in a very small voice, "because she knew we wouldn't want her to go." She gave her son a very meaningful look. "Isn't that true, Michael?"

He looked down. Was he going to have to avoid his mother's eyes for the rest of his life? "I think that's the general idea," he muttered.

"Well, it's not a very good idea," his

father harrumphed. "Ever since she met that Chris Peterson fellow, she's not exactly been overflowing with good ideas. First she doesn't want to go to college, now she doesn't want to be with her family on Christmas." He shook his head. "I don't understand her."

"Chris isn't in the picture anymore," Michael told his father, glad that there was at least something good he could tell him. "He's left town."

His father's eyebrows rose.

"In fact, that's another reason why Marianne went to New York. She's kind of brokenhearted."

"Ah . . . well," his father sighed and reached over for his hot chocolate. "A broken heart I guess I can understand."

"And she felt embarrassed about it, because she knew you and Mom didn't like Chris." He wondered just how much more he would have to lie in order to appease his father's suspicions about Marianne's unannounced departure. It seemed as if he was almost at the end of it, if his father would accept this last little piece.

His father mulled it over while he sipped his hot chocolate. Pat and Michael watched him closely until he spoke again. "I hope she doesn't stay away too long," he finally said. "I'll miss her."

Both Michael and Pat heaved sighs of relief.

"She'll be back before New Year's," Michael assured him.

"Okay." John took one last big sip of the chocolate, and then rose. "I'll go get the stepladder in the garage so we can trim the top of the tree," he announced, and then left.

An uncomfortable silence brewed between Michael and his mother, which she finally broke.

"You knew, and you didn't tell me," she accused so softly he could hardly hear her. "How could you?"

"Marianne's spending Christmas with Glenda, Mom."

"But that's not all she's doing, is it, Michael?" she cajoled him. "She's gone to New York to get an abortion, hasn't she?"

He wouldn't reply. He knew his mother was aware of the truth, even if he didn't tell her that her guess was correct. He'd promised Marianne that he'd keep the reason for her trip to New York a secret, so he shrugged his shoulders noncommittally, keeping his eyes on the mantelpiece.

Pat began to cry. "What's Glenda's telephone number? I'm going to call Marianne right now."

"I can't give you her phone number," Michael said firmly.

She turned an astonished face to him.

"I think you should leave her alone, Mom." Tenderly, he put a hand on his mother's shoulder. He felt sorry for her—he could see the pain and hurt so clearly on her face—but his first loyalty was to his sister, who needed his support more.

His mother angrily shook off his hand. "I'll call her doctor, then. I know his number. He must know what she's about to do."

Michael shrugged. "I can't stop you."

"And then I'm going to get on a plane to New York," she continued, her eyes bright with determination, "and I'm going to stop her from doing this horrible thing!"

He watched as she swept out of the room and up the stairs to the privacy of her bedroom, where she could call Marianne's doctor without his father's overhearing. He wondered if his mother hadn't told him about Marianne's pregnancy out of loyalty to his sister or because she refused to accept that an abortion might take place. If she had her way, it never would.

Michael sighed and picked up his mug of hot chocolate. As he took his first sip, he grimaced, discovering it had already gone cold.

The day before Christmas, at eleven in the morning, Pat Randolph was waiting nervously in Dr. David Gilchrist's office. Her appointment with him had been made for nine o'clock, but she hadn't been able to get there on time. Snow had continued to fall throughout the previous night so that when morning came there were drifts, some as high as the window ledges, obstructing the driveway.

When John had decided that he might just as well take a bus to work rather than spend the better part of the morning clearing the drive, Pat had bitten her tongue rather than let him know how desperate she was to get the car out. Some neighborhood boys had saved her by shoveling the driveway for a plateful of cookies, some hot chocolate, and a few dollars.

Now she was late and the receptionist told her that she'd have to wait until the doctor could squeeze her in.

She crossed her legs and folded and refolded her leather gloves in her hand, wondering if Dr. Gilchrist would be sympathetic. She'd never heard of him until she'd discovered he was Marianne's doctor. How she wished that her daughter had gone to their family doctor instead. It would be so much easier to discuss her condition with someone she knew and trusted than with a complete stranger. She hoped he would tell her what she needed to know. As the moments passed like hours, she began to wonder if she'd ever get in to see him.

Finally, a patient left and she realized she was the only one left in the waiting room. The receptionist looked up and nodded at the doctor's door. "Go ahead, Mrs. Randolph," she directed. "He'll see you now."

Pat jumped to her feet, and without even knocking, pushed into Dr. David Gilchrist's office. She hadn't completely known what she'd been expecting, but she knew it wasn't what she saw. Dr. Gilchrist wasn't the kindly, old general practitioner she'd thought he might be. He was young —young enough to have just gotten out of medical school—with light brown wavy hair and a handsome, intelligent face.

"Mrs. Randolph?" His voice was low and well modulated.

"Yes," she replied.

"Please sit down." He waved to a chair in front of his desk.

Pat sat and folded her hands in her lap. She wondered how difficult he was going to make this for her, but when she looked up, his face seemed kind and concerned. Perhaps it wasn't going to be difficult at all.

"You're here to talk about Marianne?" he asked.

She nodded.

"I have to warn you ahead of time, Mrs. Randolph, that there isn't very much I can tell you." Seeing her mouth open to protest, he put up a hand and continued. "I'm Marianne's physician and I'm bound to uphold the confidentiality of our relationship."

Her heart sank. If he wouldn't tell her what she needed to know, he couldn't be kind or concerned. "Doctor," she began, "my daughter is about to make a terrible mistake. Do you want that on your conscience?"

"Marianne made up her own mind about how she wanted to handle her situation," Dave Gilchrist replied, not being persuaded by Pat's effort to make him feel guilty. "Apparently, you don't agree with her and think it's a mistake. But isn't it her decision, not yours?"

Pat twisted her gloves in her hands. "She doesn't know what she's getting into. She doesn't know what can happen to her. She's having an abortion but she doesn't know the first thing about it—" Pat had almost blurted out, "not like I do," when she caught herself. "She'll ruin her life," she said instead, twisting her gloves even more furiously.

Dave Gilchrist raised his eyebrows. "Marianne is fine, Mrs. Randolph. She's in capable hands."

"Do you know where she is?" She leaned forward expectantly. "Please tell me, doctor. I have to know. I have to stop her."

He flushed and squirmed uneasily in his chair. "I can't tell you that."

She jumped up and began to pound on his desk. "You have to tell me!" she demanded, then fell back into the chair and burst into loud, wrenching sobs. "No one will tell me!" she cried. "You're all shutting me out of my own daughter's life."

"Mrs. Randolph," the doctor said gently as he rose and approached her chair, "please don't get so upset." He knelt next to her and patted her shoulder. "Is it so horrible?"

Mutely, she raised her head and nodded.

Dave Gilchrist looked into her eyes and knew, instantly, that her emotions on the matter were not inconsequential ones. Within the depths of her blue eyes, he saw a fear and a sadness so overwhelming that he almost felt it himself. Whatever Pat Randolph's reasons were for wanting to prevent her daughter's abortion, he knew they came from the depths of her soul.

"We have to stop her," she whispered, sensing that he understood at last. "Please."

As if he were in a daze, he nodded his head and returned to his desk. "She's in New York," he said, leafing through his address book and writing the address down on a slip of paper. "Here." He handed it to Pat.

She took the piece of paper, looked at the address, and then slipped it into her purse. "You'll come with me, won't you?" she begged. "I don't think I can go alone."

"What about your husband?" Dave asked. "Isn't he the logical one to go?"

"He doesn't know," Pat confessed. "Marianne has sworn me to secrecy, so I can't tell him. My son refuses to interfere, so he won't go." She turned her lovely face up to Dave, lovely in spite of the redness around her eyes and the tears that still glistened as they trailed down her cheekbones. "I'm all alone."

Dave swallowed. To go with her to New York to try to prevent his own patient from doing what she felt she had to do was something he knew he should, and had to, refuse. It was unethical.

But he'd already ignored ethics when he'd given Marianne's mother the address of the abortion clinic. He had just faced his first moral crisis as a doctor and had failed miserably.

He slumped in his chair and stared down at his hands, all the while feeling the heat of Pat's anxious gaze. Inwardly, he groaned. No matter what his training had taught him, no matter what his better instincts were telling him to do, he knew he was going to do exactly the opposite. Something extremely powerful had touched him when he'd looked into Pat Randolph's eyes, something that had more power over him than his medical training or his common sense.

"Yes, I'll go with you," he replied, his human emotions defeating all his doctor's logic. He straightened up in his chair, grabbed the phone receiver, and dialed the airport to find out when the first flight to New York would be.

Pat stood up and approached his desk. "Thank you," she said, beginning to cry again. "Oh, thank you so much."

Chapter Eleven
The Past Revealed

Christmas Eve and Day had been a nightmare. Because of the snow, all flights out of Bay City had been canceled. Pat had been trapped at home with John and all their relatives, waiting for Dave Gilchrist to call and tell her when they'd be able to leave for New York.

Perhaps the delay had been for the best, though; it would have been much more difficult to explain to John why she was joining Marianne in New York and abandoning him at Christmas. When Dave called to inform her that they'd be able to fly out first thing in the morning of the twenty-sixth, it was easy to tell John that she missed her daughter and thought she might join her in New York for a little post-Christmas sale shopping.

John, noticing how subdued and quiet his wife had been all through the holidays, had agreed eagerly, hoping that a change of scene would improve her mood.

"Kiss Marianne for me, won't you?" he instructed after he kissed Pat good-bye before leaving for work. "And tell her she was very bad to leave and not tell us."

"Yes, John," Pat murmured, distracted. If he didn't leave soon he was going to be there when the doctor arrived to drive her to the airport. How would she explain that?

"And, Pat," he said softly, putting a hand under her chin and tipping it up so her eyes met his, "cheer up." He didn't like what he saw in his wife's eyes lately. Except for that one day before Christmas, they had been unaccountably filled with a deep sadness that he felt powerless to change. "I love you," he murmured, and kissed her gently on the lips.

"Me, too," Pat whispered. Her eyes began to fill with tears. "Now, off to work." She shooed him out the door before he could see her crying.

A few minutes later, as she stood by the parlor window looking out to the street in anxious anticipation, she saw Dave pull up. Without even waiting for him to get out of the car, she picked up her carry-on bag and purse, threw on her winter-white coat, and flew out the door.

He was halfway up the walk to the front door when she met him.

He took her bag. "Ready?"

She nodded wordlessly.

"Did you get Glenda's folks' address?" he asked as he opened the car door for her.

"Yes, Michael finally gave it to me." It had taken a while, but she'd finally managed to get it out of him after Christmas Day dinner. Since she already had the clinic's address, he hadn't seen much sense in withholding Glenda's anymore.

Dave got into the driver's seat and started the car. "He's very loyal to his sister, isn't he?" He knew that Michael thought his mother was interfering in Marianne's life and didn't want to get involved.

"Yes, he is," she agreed. "They're twins, so naturally they've always been close."

He pulled out into the street and began the trip to the airport. "That must have been hard on you at times," he observed. "You must have felt shut out."

Pat turned to him, surprised at how perceptive he was. "Yes, I did. I still do," she amended. "A mother likes to feel close to her children, so it's difficult when she sometimes feels her children are closer to each other than to her."

"It's not intentional, though," Dave interjected. "It's just that the bond between twins is very special, and very strong."

Pat raised her eyebrows. "You sound as if you know," she remarked.

He laughed. "My older brothers are twins. I always felt shut out when we were growing up. They ganged up on me, and they ganged up on my parents."

Now Pat laughed. She began to tell Dave some stories about Michael and Marianne and the scrapes they'd gotten into when they were children. She forgot, for the time being, why she was going to New York with this handsome doctor and what awaited her there when she stepped off the plane.

It wasn't until they were finally in the air and leaving Bay City far behind that she had time to reflect on why she was taking this trip. She stared out the window at the city she had grown up in, married in, borne her children in, and would probably die in. As it grew smaller and smaller until it was only a faint green patch on the horizon, memories began to unreel.

There should be a saying that goes: "Like mother, like daughter," Pat mused. Because what was Marianne's story, was also her own, just twenty or so years removed. Pat knew only too well what an abortion could do to a woman. The truth was, she had had one herself under circumstances frighteningly similar to Marianne's. That was why she had to stop her daughter from coming to the same fate: her abortion hadn't been the end of something, it had only been the beginning of a long, horrible nightmare.

Pat shivered. It had been so long since she'd been forced to think of those days. She had hoped she'd never have to again.

Dave noticed her shivering, the frown that crossed her face, and the look of sadness that followed shortly after. "Would you feel better if you talked about it?" he asked gently. "I'm a good listener."

She looked down at her hands, usually so well groomed. Her cuticles were ragged and her nails bitten to the quick. Nerves. Perhaps what she needed was someone to talk to, someone sympathetic like Dave Gilchrist seemed to be. How often during the past weeks had she wanted to talk to John, had she needed to talk to him, but Marianne's vow of secrecy had made it impossible. She'd had to bear all this pain on her own.

"I really am," Dave repeated, and took one of her hands in his. It wasn't a provocative gesture as some men might have made it. It was merely a gesture of friendly compassion.

She pulled the white mink collar of her coat closer. "If I only knew where to begin."

"Begin at the beginning," he said, giving her hand a squeeze, and then letting it go. "That's usually the best place."

The beginning. Pat began. "When I was eighteen I fell in love with a young man. He was handsome and smart and his family knew my family. Everyone thought we would be married. But one night we got carried away and we made love. I hated myself for it the next day." Her hand balled into a fist in her lap. "But Tom—Tom Baxter was his name—he didn't hate himself. He wanted to continue what we'd started. He said we were going to be married anyway, so what did it matter?"

Pat gulped. "But it mattered. I got pregnant. When I told Tom he refused to have anything to do with me. He said it was my own fault for not being smart enough to protect myself!" She was surprised at how much old feelings could still hurt. Pausing for a moment, she collected herself, then went on. "He made me get an abortion. He said if I tried to keep the baby he'd spread rumors that he hadn't been the only one I'd slept with, that I'd been sleeping with other boys and had no idea who the father of my baby was."

"What a horrible thing to say." Dave hadn't been expecting a story like this from the woman sitting next to him. She was so ladylike, so genteel, he never would have guessed anything this ugly had once happened in her life. Her words held him spellbound.

"It was a horrible thing to say, and I

believed he'd do it, too." She leaned her head back as if she was suddenly weary. "I was so frightened I couldn't see any way out. I arranged to have an abortion. It was in a trailer behind a diner on the outskirts of town. I'll never forget the shaky, dirty table I had to lie on, or the ugly little man who performed it, or the way he looked at me as if I were dirty, too."

"It's not like that anymore. If you're worried about Marianne because of that, please don't," he reassured her.

She didn't even seem to hear him. "It was a bad job. I became infected and nearly died. The doctors told me I'd be sterile for the rest of my life." Pat shook her head. "Thank God they were wrong."

He squeezed her hand.

Looking out the window, she saw they were above the clouds now and she gazed at the surreal terrain beneath her. Instead of houses and little patches of green, she now saw mountains and valleys made of clouds, brilliantly white under a sky that was so blue it almost hurt to look at it. Her mind wandered back. . . .

When she'd finally recovered enough to leave the hospital, her parents had taken her home. Jim and Mary Matthews were good, honest people, stanchions of Bay City society, and nothing like this had ever happened in either of their families. They'd liked Tom Baxter and had thought he was going to make a fine husband for their daughter. They couldn't understand why he had acted as he did, and they forbade her to see him again.

But one day, shortly after she'd returned from the hospital, feeling as if she'd go mad if she stayed cooped up in the house any longer, Pat disobeyed her parents. She slipped out of the house and went to see Tom. There were some things she had to say to him.

When he opened the door to find her there, his handsome face had turned ugly. "What are you doing here?" he barked.

She pushed past him and stood her ground. "I want to talk to you." Still not feeling all that sure on her feet, she had to grasp the back of a chair to steady herself.

"I thought we'd said everything," Tom replied, closing the door when he realized she wasn't going to leave.

"You said what you wanted to say, but I haven't said what I want to say," she told him, stubbornly.

"Look, Pat," he said, leaning against the door, "I thought you understood I didn't want to see you anymore. We're through."

Rage began to build within her. "I nearly died, Tom. I nearly died getting rid of the baby you refused to take any responsibility for."

"So?" He shrugged. "What am I supposed to do now?" He walked over to the window, pulled the curtain aside, and gazed outside as if ignoring her would make her go away. "Forget about it," he advised, turning back from the view. "Find someone else."

"Forget about it!" Pat cried. "I'll never be able to have a child and all you can say is 'Forget about it'!" She hated him. A black feeling surged within her, and she could feel it take over her senses as if she were no longer in control of them.

"Well, you'll never have to have another abortion now, will you?" he retorted with a smirk.

As if an unseen hand were pushing her forward, she approached him with rage in her eyes. "You can't do this to me," she said slowly, her hands raising and balling into fists.

"I already have," he replied offhandedly. "And there's not a damn thing you can do about it."

With a scream, Pat attacked him. Her fists pummeled him with all the rage and anger she felt within. He was too surprised to fight back. Grabbing on to the curtain, he tried to pull it between them, but she ripped it away and struck his face over and over again with her fists.

"Stop it!" he cried. "Pat!" Somehow he pulled himself away from her and ran to the door. His face was already bloodied; one of her punches must have produced a gash in his lip because blood was dripping from his mouth. "Get out of here!" he yelled.

Wordlessly, she turned and saw what she had done. Dear Lord, she'd never hit anyone before in her life! She began to cry in loud, wrenching sobs.

"Shut up!" he commanded. "Do you want everyone to know what you've done?" He put a hand up to his face, and when he pulled it away, saw the blood on his fingers. "My God, you've drawn blood."

She began to cry even harder. She couldn't stop the sobs that just seemed to well up and push out of her, as if they were some kind of wild animal struggling to be free.

"Shut up," he repeated, with a menacing gleam in his eye. He approached her now, his hand raised.

Pat looked up just in time to see his hand descending to hit her. And then he slapped her over and over again, each time telling her to shut up. She thought he'd kill her before she could get away. His eyes were like a cougar's moving in for the kill.

Desperate, Pat looked around her for something with which to fend him off. She yanked a vase off a table and held it up. "Leave me alone!" she begged.

But he was too far gone to even hear her. His slapping had turned into punches all over her body, and then he was grabbing her and trying to throw her to the floor.

Pat was sure he'd kill her if he got her down. She raised the vase as high as she could and smashed it into the side of his head.

She would never forget the look of surprise she saw on his face as he stumbled under the impact, but she didn't see him fall. As soon as his hands released her, she pulled away, turned, and ran out the door. . . .

"What happened to Tom?" she heard Dave Gilchrist ask, as if he were very far away.

Pulled out of her thoughts, she had to pause for a moment or two to reorient herself. Her memory had been so powerful, she had felt as if she'd been there, reliving the horror all over again. "He died," she whispered. "And I stood trial for his murder."

She explained to Dave the scene she had just relived. "The police arrived shortly afterward. Some neighbors had called because they'd heard me scream. I'd left in such a rush I'd forgotten my purse. I was their only suspect and I was willing to confess. I thought I had killed him."

And now she recalled the long nightmare of the trial. "My parents hired the best lawyer they could find for me. He

worked day and night to try to come up
with a case for my acquittal. The best he
could do was have me plead temporary
insanity."

"What was the trial like for you? It must
have been ghastly." Dave couldn't believe
that the beautiful, fragile-seeming woman
next to him had managed to emerge from
all this as unscarred as she appeared to me.

"It was like a carnival," Pat said. "The
courtroom was packed every day. People
couldn't get enough of it. And everything
came out: my affair with Tom, the abortion, my sickness. The only way I could get
through it was to pretend that it was
happening to someone else. Sometimes I'd
just tell myself that it was a bad dream that
I would awaken from. If it hadn't been for
my parents and my lawyer, I never would
have made it."

"You would have made it," he assured
her. "You're a lot stronger than you think
you are. You have to have been to survive
what you did." He wondered how, having
known her for such a short amount of
time, he could be so sure of his words. But
he was. Pat Randolph had no idea just how
strong, and beautiful, she was. "How did
the trial go?" he asked.

Pat shrugged. "It was a standard murder
trial, I'm told. The prosecutor tried to
convince the jury that I had killed Tom in
cold blood. My lawyer told them that I was

a victim, that Tom had just used me, and when I became inconvenient, tossed me away."

"Which was true."

"Yes," she admitted, "but still Tom Baxter was dead. Did he deserve to be?"

Dave didn't know what to say.

"The final witness was the medical examiner who'd done the autopsy on Tom's body. The prosecution thought they had incontrovertible evidence that he had died from a blow to the head. They assumed it was from when I hit him with the vase. But my lawyer discovered that the blow that caused his death was on the right side of his head."

Dave raised his eyebrows, not understanding her flow of logic.

"I'm right-handed. I had to have struck him on the left side. Apparently, after I left, Tom must have stumbled into a table and hit his head on the edge. That's what caused his death. I hadn't killed him after all."

"And so you were acquitted," Dave surmised.

"The charges of first-degree murder were dropped, and I was charged with assault. But because it was in self-defense, John won my acquittal."

"John?" he said, puzzled. "Isn't that your husband's name?"

Pat nodded slowly. "We were married

shortly afterward. He was my knight in shining armor," she said softly with a small laugh.

"And you lived happily ever after," Dave completed the story.

"By and large." She turned her face away to the clouds and the sky out the windows. Already, she felt as if she'd said much too much to Dave. He didn't need to know that her marriage was like most in its ups and downs, perhaps even more tumultuous than most. Right now it was having one of its downs.

Dave was silent for quite a while. "And now there's Marianne," he finally said, as if he were talking to himself.

Pat sighed. Her beautiful daughter, Marianne, whom she'd tried to protect from everything bad in the world so she'd never have to go through what she had. And here she was, in a similar predicament. "Perhaps I overprotected her," Pat said, "just as my parents overprotected me. Maybe it's better if you just let your children do as they want and make their own mistakes and learn from them. If I hadn't been so naive, maybe I could have seen what kind of boy Tom Baxter was. Maybe Marianne could have done the same with Chris."

"That's a lot of 'maybes,'" Dave remarked.

"I suppose so," Pat conceded. "But I don't want Marianne to make the same mistake I made. There aren't many days that pass that I don't think of that baby, the baby that was Tom's and mine. I should have had that child. I should never have had the abortion."

"You say that now," he began, but Pat cut him off.

"I say that now because what I did was wrong, and not because it caused me so much pain and heartache, but because it was basically a selfish thing to do. I wasn't thinking of the child. I was only thinking of myself."

"And now you think Marianne is only thinking of herself?" Dave asked gently. "Maybe she's also thinking of you and her father and the rest of your family. And the child. Illegitimacy isn't any different from when you were a young girl, Pat. It's still a stigma. People still talk."

Pat was very quiet next to him.

"I don't mean to be hard on you, Pat. I hardly know you. But do you think you might be unfair in asking Marianne to do something you couldn't do yourself?"

She was cut to the quick by his question. Was she asking too much of her daughter? Was she being unfair? "I don't know," she admitted, finally. "I honestly don't know."

The sign to fasten their seat belts blinked on above them. They were ready to make their descent to New York City.

"I just hope I have the chance to ask her

that before it's too late," she said to Dave, as they buckled up.

They both looked out the window. Beneath them, the Statue of Liberty stood proud and lonely in New York harbor. Then they were passing over Central Park as the plane turned and dipped lower and lower on its approach to the airport.

Pat crossed her fingers. Would they make it in time? Or would Marianne have already decided her fate?

Next to her, Dave Gilchrist crossed his fingers, too. He wasn't quite sure what he was wishing for, only that the woman next to him, and her daughter, would find some peace between themselves.

That wasn't too much to hope for, was it?